WHAT READERS LOVE ABOUT *THE PASSION OF JUDAS*

"I loved every word from start to finish, and look forward to more from this Author.

"'The Passion of Judas' is a realistic, if fictional, adaptation of how events of the bible in the times of Jesus may have happened. Craig's attention to historical facts sets the scene for an intriguing story of betrayal, romance and above all trust.

This is well worth the read.."

I0593655

Titles by Robin Craig

The Hunter Series

Frankensteel

The Geneh War

Time Enough for Killing

Leonardo's Child

Time Travel and Alternative History

The Time Surgeons

Hannibal's Witch

The Passion of Judas

Short Stories

Past, Present Future

Non-Fiction Philosophy

Dialogue on the Two Chief World Systems

Good Without God

Cloning Around: The Ethics of Human Cloning and Stem Cell
Research

For the latest news visit robin-craig.com or follow on
fb.me/authorcraig

The Passion of Judas

ROBIN CRAIG

Published by ThoughtWare Books.

Available from Amazon.com and other retail outlets.
Available on Kindle and other devices.

Cover art by Kira Craig using images from Pixabay with fonts from 1001 Fonts.

Author's website: robin-craig.com

ISBN 978-0-9803205-1-0

History belongs to the victors, legends to the people,
fantasy to literature. — Péter Esterházy

CONTENTS

MAP OF ROMAN JUDAEA

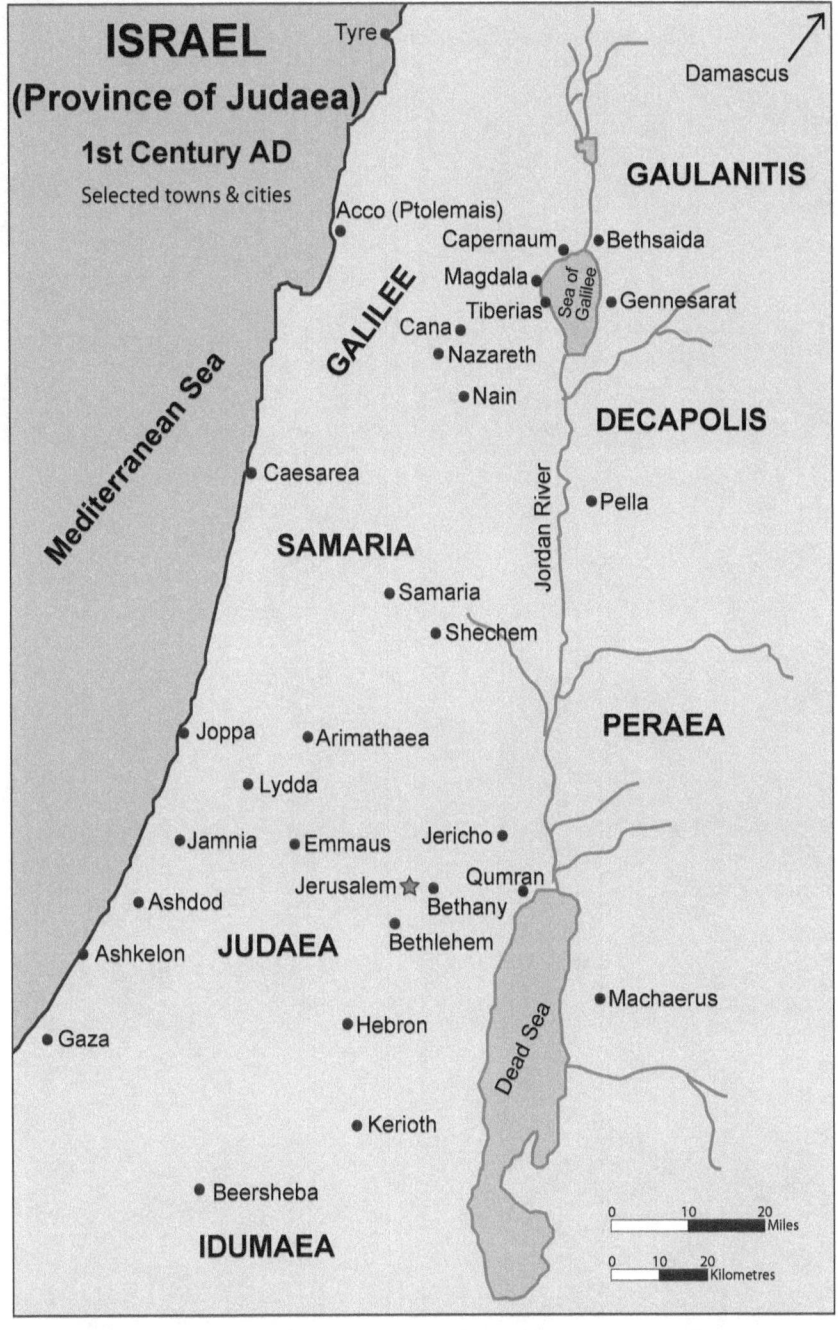

ISRAEL
(Province of Judaea)
1st Century AD
Selected towns & cities

Tyre
Damascus

GAULANITIS

Acco (Ptolemais)

GALILEE

Capernaum • Bethsaida

Magdala •
Sea of Galilee
Tiberias •
Cana •
Nazareth • Gennesarat

Nain

DECAPOLIS

Mediterranean Sea

Caesarea

Jordan River

Pella

SAMARIA

Samaria

Shechem

Joppa

Arimathaea

PERAEA

Lydda

Jamnia • Emmaus

Jericho •

Jerusalem ☆
Bethany

Qumran

Ashdod

Bethlehem

Ashkelon   JUDAEA

Dead Sea

Machaerus

Gaza

Hebron

Kerioth

Beersheba

IDUMAEA

0   10   20
Miles

0   10   20
Kilometres

PREFACE

The story of Jesus Christ is a dramatic tale of religious controversy, political manoeuvring, ambition, love and betrayal: but little is known for sure about what really happened nearly two millennia ago. The only sources are the Gospels of the New Testament, each written with its author's agenda in mind and each giving rather different accounts.

If we read the Gospels without preconceptions they come across as collections of anecdotes strung together into a single narrative, with the tales in different Gospels having taken different routes and final forms. This leads to one of the premises of this novel: the Gospels provide clues to the truth not the truth itself. Behind the stories is a reality but those stories diverged, changed and amplified in the telling—as stories spread person to person do.

So how do we strip off the layers of myth to reach the reality?

It is a difficult task. It is not even certain that Jesus lived at all: perhaps the Gospels do not record his life but are simply "back stories": anecdotes about various itinerant preachers comingled to explain and justify a religion that had already emerged from the melting pot of Mystery and Messianic sects of first century Judea.

However that would make a poor novel, and for the sake of this story I have assumed that the basic events and characters were real.

But who were they, really? Judas Iscariot and Mary Magdalene were two of Jesus' most important disciples, yet their characters, roles and motivations are more hinted at than revealed. All the Gospels tell us about Judas is his name, that he was close enough to be trusted with the money, yet he betrayed Jesus. There is nothing about why he followed Jesus in the first place, what caused his estrangement, or why he betrayed Jesus for so little (thirty pieces of silver was barely more than a month's wages for a laborer of the time). Even the stories of his death are inconsistent: was he racked with guilt, throwing his silver back at the priests before hanging himself (Matthew 27); or did he cheerfully buy a field with his silver then fall headlong onto it so his bowels burst onto the ground (Acts 1)?

For her part Mary Magdalene has a disproportionate number of mentions, watched the crucifixion and was reported to be the first witness to the Resurrection. But little is said about her personally except Jesus had cast demons out of her and she helped support him. Some identify her with the woman caught in adultery, others as Jesus' wife. Yet after she witnesses the Resurrection, surely the most crucial event in Christendom—she vanishes entirely from the record.

Such hints of importance in the presence of gaping holes in the narrative prick up a detective's ears and give innumerable "what ifs" to the novelist. Hence this novel was born.

A note on names: In this novel most place names retain the forms familiar to modern readers, but for historical flavor personal names are closer to their original dialects. Some will be obvious, but part of the pleasure of reading this book is ascertaining who is who. The *Glossary of Names* at the end includes translations of names, but as it includes spoilers it is best to leave it until the end.

My thanks go to historian Dr Michael Affleck for reading a draft of this book and commenting on aspects of Roman history; however any errors remain my own.

~~~

The quote beginning this book is *History belongs to the victors, legends to the people, fantasy to literature.* That is my other guide to interpreting the Gospels. So if this novel challenges your beliefs and opens your eyes to other possibilities of what really happened all those centuries ago— I have succeeded.

But is it true?

It might be.

<div align="right">

Robin Craig
January 2016

</div>

PROLOGUE

He watched from the shadows, fingering his blade. He could see her, pushed roughly to the ground, clothes dusty and torn. He could see the crowd around her, angry in their mutterings, self-righteous in their rage.

His lips curled in contempt, baring his teeth in his own anger. For there was something else he could see in the crowd: the sly eyes, darting in poorly concealed hunger, in the faces of the men who would condemn her. Condemn her even as their own eyes were drawn to her naked breasts, only partly hidden by her ripped clothes, though she tried so desperately to cover them in futile modesty. Breasts whose soft swelling he knew so well yet so briefly; whose soft form the hypocrites of the town lusted over even as they planned to crush the life from the soul that gave them warmth.

But it was her eyes he saw most clearly, filled with fear and pleading for a mercy that would not come. The light was still bright outside and the people on the street could not see him. But if she could see him, he knew her eyes would turn to a contempt and loathing even greater than his own for the men of the town. *Coward*, they would say. *Betrayer*, they would accuse. *Liar*, they would damn.
Judas.

CHAPTER 1: A BOY, LIKE ANY OTHER

He remembered the warmth, the darkness, the thumping beat. He remembered the heaving, screaming transition into a world of lights, shapes and startlingly sharp sounds. Soon he would remember none of it, for now that new world was all his world. The light changed from bright to dim to bright again; colors and shapes danced before his eyes; he felt cold and heat, cloth and wind. And he drank the warm liquid from his mother, and slept in contentment. In that he was no different from any other boy.

He grew, as boys did: taller, straighter and stronger as the years moved past. There was nothing overly remarkable about him. His eyes were dark; his hair also dark with a touch of russet, as if the red sands that sometimes flew with the wind had made him theirs; his skin tanned by the burning sun of his land. He was perhaps faster than most: a quick runner and even quicker of wit; perhaps that is why he was more cynical than most. If he had any peculiar talent, it was a certain holistic understanding of patterns: he would see the whole fabric of events or circumstances without being too distracted by the details, and go straight to the essence of a problem or the weakness of his opponents in a game. Had he been born of a Patrician family in Rome he might have become a great general; had he been of more violent temperament he might have become one in his own land and fought, and probably died, in battle against one of those Roman aristocrats. But he was neither.

He believed in the God of his fathers, as they all did: for why would they question it? But perhaps he believed with less intensity and more questioning; perhaps he chafed more at the invaders who ruled his land with iron; wondered more how the God before whom his people prostrated themselves could allow such impositions upon those who gave Him their devotion. As men they were no better than other men: no freer from anger, lust and lies; but nor were they worse, so why did their God single them out for His punishments? It was not that the gods of the invaders were stronger than theirs. He knew that: the God of the Hebrews was Almighty. *El Shaddai*, the Lord of Hosts. All other gods were false gods, things of stone and wood without life or power, or demons deceiving those whom God had not chosen.

So it had to be punishment. But the boy could not understand why. Nor could his elders explain it. It was their burden to bear, for God was both just and wise beyond the understanding of mortal men. Had the boy been able to look into the minds of other men, perhaps he would have found more doubts than he could see in their words and faces. Perhaps if he had been like other men his doubts would have been buried; or perhaps hidden, the conflict expressing itself in an ever more strident and judgmental spirit: the greater the inner doubt refracting into the more pious the exterior. But this boy was not like that. If he did not express his doubts, nor did he bury them: he kept them in a private place, where he would occasionally visit them, examine them and wonder.

But if all boys are unique, in other ways they are all the same. This boy's uniqueness was not the kind that would shake the Earth and declare, "Here is one to watch!" Had one of the invaders taken a dislike to him he could have ended the boy's life with one stroke of a sword. His father, mother and brothers would have mourned, but known they could do nothing beyond mourning. They would curse the Romans, but not their God. They would curse the Romans to their God, but the man who killed their son would live on exactly as he had before. As would the world, neither knowing nor caring about his passing, any more than it had about his existence.

But no man of Rome took such a dislike to him, or if he did the boy was too fast and the man's anger too brief. Or perhaps all the boys of Judah looked the same to him. In any case there were not many Romans here. There was a garrison in the town, but his neighborhood on its outskirts was unimportant; the invaders more a threat like storm clouds over the mountains than a constant and present danger. Those who passed through were arrogant and casual in their brutality, but his family was not important enough to draw their attention. The boy knew his scriptures and through them some of the past, or at least the past as filtered through the prejudices of those who had written the scriptures; sometimes he wondered if perhaps life was less brutal under the invaders than it would have been without them. But the boy did not know, and even if he had known it was beyond his power to alter.

What questions he had were questions for nights, illnesses or anger. They were not the focus of his life. Perhaps they would have been if his family were of the priesthood, or wealthy merchants who sent their sons to learn at the feet of savants. But his family were simple and his life was just a boy's life: obeying his parents, doing what work he was able to, playing with his friends and brothers, and when he found the opportunity roaming through the pastures, scrublands and deserts surrounding his home town. That could have been as fatal as stealing from a Roman: a snake could kill as easily and possibly more painfully than a sword, and the rare wild beast take a boy and leave no clue to his fate beyond bloody rags. But those dangers too he avoided. And so he lived on, like most though not all of his companions.

Then the day came when perhaps he could get answers to his questions. He was approaching the age of maturity. This always involved ceremony, marking the imminent passing of boyhood and initiation into the mysteries of the world of manhood. But while his parents were simple they had worked hard, and if the boy was of sharp wits at least some of them had come from his father. He had husbanded his money carefully, with one eye on the present and the other on the future. So as they had done for each of their sons in turn, as he approached his twelfth year they hopefully counted their hidden savings and confirmed that at last, for this lucky son, they had money to spare. Perhaps the money could have been better spent or better saved. But his father and mother believed in their God with the devotion of those who knew no better and hoped that devotion brought rewards. It was a journey not without price and dangers. But a journey to the seat of the ancient kingdom was dear to the hearts of all believers.

Their boy would be inducted into adulthood by the priests of the Temple itself.

They were going to Jerusalem.

~~~

The boy looked around in awe. Jerusalem was like nothing he had ever seen, and entering it a transition perhaps even greater than his long-forgotten birth. Like his home town it had buildings, people and animals. But the scale! The noise and bustle of so much humanity and its accompaniments was literally staggering. The smell of animals, their sweat and dung, was familiar, but at this scale almost overwhelming. The whole family looked around, open-mouthed, occasionally hustled along by curses from those more inured to its glory.

They found an inn, some distance from the Temple compound and not expensive. His father disappeared for some time, finding his way to the Temple to make the arrangements. Neither his journey nor his request were unusual, and the wonderment of the father in being so near the Earthly presence of his God was matched by the boredom of the junior Levite to whom he was finally shunted. Still, the Levite was a dedicated man and his boredom did not show. There were other boys here for the same reason; they would all be examined by the priests in two days' time.

For all his excitement about his upcoming meeting with the mysterious Priests of God Most High, the boy was still a boy: and his excitement at two days free in such a city was if anything greater. A younger boy might have been afraid; but to a boy edging into manhood, and especially this boy, the sights, sounds and smells of such a place, and the sheer magnitude of it, were a revelation of magnificence he had never dreamed of.

Boys, especially boys excited by new sights, are not known for their careful prudence. And so this boy found himself running through a crowded street, but as he ran around a corner encountering another boy doing much the same thing in the opposite direction. The result of the collision, besides tangles of limbs and sharply exhaled breaths, were two boys bottom down in the dirt of the street, looking at each other in rather comical surprise.

"Watch where you're going, you idiot!" they both cried simultaneously. Then they sat back staring at each other, and both burst out laughing.

In his accustomed rapid way the boy leapt to his feet, chuckling, and put out his hand to the other. "Yehuda, son of Shimon, of Kerioth", he said. The other boy took his hand with a grin and pulled himself out of the dirt. "Yeshua, son of Yossef, of Nazareth."

The boys looked at each other, still gripping hands, taking each other's measure. Yehuda found himself drawn into the other's eyes, drowning in their perception. In most ways the other boy, Yeshua, was as unremarkable as Yehuda himself: poured from the same mold; skin a shade lighter, muscles and calluses a shade harder, perhaps indicating more labor with tools under more cover than in Yehuda's existence. But his dark eyes seemed almost preternaturally observant, as if seeing not the body of the boy before him, but into his soul and beyond. What he saw there, he did not say.

"You are a long way from home, clumsy stranger," said Yehuda.

"As are you, reckless boy."

"I am here with my parents, for my *bar mitzvah*."

"As am I."

Then the other boy grinned.

"So! You are named after our people, and I after he who led them into this land. Perhaps this is a sign. Perhaps one day you will follow me, as our people once followed Yeshua into the Promised Land!"

Yehuda grinned back, releasing his hand. "Follow you? How can I follow you, when I am in front of you?" And with that, he spun and ran into the crowds; after a second's delay, Yeshua chased after him, yelling. A stall owner cursed as first one boy then the other hurtled past him on either side, almost upsetting his tray of olives into the dirt.

"Boys!" he muttered in irritation, albeit somewhat leavened by the memories of his own boyhood. "They're all the same!"

CHAPTER 2: BECOMING MEN

The boys were divided into small groups for their examination by the priests. Whether the boys were divided at random or according to some ritual formula was not imparted to the boys; in any case, when Yehuda looked around for this new friend, Yeshua was nowhere to be seen.

Some of the boys faced their questioners nervously, but Yehuda was confident in his knowledge; whatever private reservations he may have had about the mysteries of his faith he knew their formalisms. Nerves or no, all of the boys were excited by the promise of the coming mysteries of adulthood. The examination was rigorous but kindly; the priests did not want to prevent these boys from becoming men, but to guide them into becoming men worthy of their God. So before long even the most nervous boys had forgotten their doubts.

Then a strange thing happened. Another priest hurried in and whispered in the ear of Yehuda's examiner. The man looked up, startled, and the two had a muttered conversation, which the boys strained but failed to here.

"Wait here," said their priest, as he hurried from the room. He did not return. Instead, a younger Levite entered the room and continued where his senior had left off. His entry silenced the curious buzzing among the boys but did not silence the questions buzzing about in their brains.

They learned more at the ceremony that night. The whispered conversations were that one of the boys had confounded the priests with his knowledge and the unorthodox but unanswerable nature of his questions. It was as if he wished to question the very foundations of their religion, yet had an abiding love and understanding of it. They could neither condemn him nor answer him. They had taken him aside and discoursed with him at length. So much so that even they, so often slaves to ritual, had forgotten the time and the proprieties. It was not until his father Yossef turned up at the entrance to the temple, frantic for news of the son who had not returned, that they realized their error and released him.

The rumors were neither hard to believe nor their object hard to identify: Yeshua found himself drawn off from the other boys by a mass of priests and scribes, like a jar of honey abducted by a swarm of flies. So much was obvious truth to the eyes of all present, but other rumors grew on them as if the flies had laid eggs. One even whispered that Yeshua's father claimed descent from King David himself, the mighty warrior who had slain the Philistine Goliath and so ushered in the golden age of the Jewish kings. Yehuda was young enough to be impudent and old enough to understand the lusts of men: an understanding amplified, if made less accurate, by his recent time with so many boys nearing manhood and looking forward to discovering such lusts themselves.

"I would not be surprised if half of Judea were descended from the old King and his many conquests," he joked to the boy who transmitted this rumor—careful that only the boys, and not the elders, could hear this observation. And, he thought, that wasn't even counting the progeny of David's even more concubine-encrusted son, Solomon.

Privately, Yehuda hoped that Yossef would keep such claims to himself, lest Herod believe him and act as kings had since time immemorial when faced with even distant pretenders to their throne.

Yehuda looked at his friend speculatively, trying to reconcile the boy who had chased him through the streets with the vaguely Messianic implications of his wisdom and lineage. Somehow Yeshua felt those speculative eyes upon him and looked up, granting his erstwhile friend a grin and a shrug: whatever wisdom the Levites saw in him, he was still a boy.

He was also still human, and even he had to be released on occasion to serve the needs of the flesh. On his way back, Yehuda ran into him, less literally this time, and inspected him speculatively.

"Ho! So there is a sage in our midst! Perhaps yesterday in the street

I should have prostrated myself, and dusted off your Royal Bum with my unworthy raiment!"

Yeshua regally stretched out his hand. "Tut, tut, Yehuda. I find your impudence—distressing. But merely kiss my hand, and your impertinence will be forgiven."

Yehuda grinned back. "I shall do that: on the day I decide to follow you!"

Yeshua looked back solemnly. "Perhaps you will, my friend; perhaps you will. Or perhaps your kiss will mark the end of it, not the beginning."

With that he tossed his head in mock arrogance and sauntered away. Yehuda looked on after him, wondering at his meaning. *I have known you but a day, a stranger met in a street: so what is this bond I feel between us? Tomorrow we leave for our homes, you north to Galilee and I toward the south; and I shall never see you again.*

But he wondered even at that.

Chapter 3: Life and Death

Yehuda went back to his home and back to his life. His father had numerous children, of whom Yehuda was neither the oldest nor the youngest. He could have stayed, serving his father, seeking a wife, and settling down in the town of his birth. But there was nothing particular to hold him there, and too much curiosity lived in his mind for him to simply settle into it because it was there.

In his eighteenth year a caravan passed through the town. Many others had passed through before. But something about this one caught his attention. Whether it was the exotic goods it carried, the quick wit of the hard man who headed it, or merely the collision of his age, hormones and opportunity he could not have said. But he spoke to the men of the caravan, and it was set.

And so he said farewell to his father, his mother, his brothers: and joined the caravan, paying his way by helping with whatever odd or dirty jobs those with more seniority or coin asked of him. He was a man of Judea, and he feared neither hard times nor hard work. But the caravan was not his life, only a means to find one.

The caravan was the life of its owner, Ananias. He was a tall, strong man, hard of eye and muscle; a long scar down is face attested to the occasional violence of his life. His caravan circled around Israel, travelling from city to town to city, transferring goods from their places of greatest supply to their places of greatest demand, with a handy premium of coin ending up in the hands of their carrier.

This made him a wealthy man, but not so wealthy he could yet surrender his caravan and spend the rest of his days popping grapes and olives into his mouth in the shade of his rooftop garden. There were many expenses in running such an operation: the purchase and upkeep of the numerous camels and asses that bore his goods, the pay of the men who drove the beasts, the reserves needed to buy whatever rare items opportunity brought his way, the upkeep of his household at home including servants skilled and reliable enough to act in his absence, and the occasional loss of all or part of some goods due to weather, weevils or other misadventure.

His one extravagance was one of the reasons Yehuda had been drawn to his caravan: the man had acquired a horse. A wealthy Roman might well have turned up his extensive nose at the beast, but in this land and for this lifestyle the wiry steed was well suited. Nor was it truly an extravagance. Caravans made a tempting target for robbers, the human wolves who made a living off the sweat of others. A hard man with a long sword riding a horse would help dissuade all but the most desperate brigands.

That was not his only defense. The men who drove the animals were all armed and trained, more or less, in the arts of fighting. Their weapons, not hidden but glinting in the sun, had allowed the caravan to pass by many robber scouts without incident. Those cases where desperation, folly or over-confidence had overcome caution had generally been short affairs ending in the deaths of one or two robbers before the rest had realized their error and vanished back to their lairs. Unfortunately they sometimes also involved the death or injury of some men of the caravan, another expense that had to be factored into the profitability of the enterprise.

Ananias also varied his route. Part of that was necessity: some supply or demand was seasonal, plus he always had his ear to the ground in any town they stopped at to learn any hints of opportunities. But part was that he knew a pattern was like a beacon to the more sophisticated bands of robbers. Far better to never travel the same route at the same time at the cost of a few days' delay than to shorten the trip but never complete it.

But as much as Ananias desired to keep his goods and his life, robbers desired the goods of any who passed through their territory: the lives of their current owners purely optional.

~~~

Yehuda was walking along in the heat, the morning sun already beating down from a sky that held no mercy, only a small hazing of dust. For the moment no tasks awaited him except keeping his ears open for any shouted commands, so he merely walked beside one of the donkeys, flicking at flies with a slender stick in counterpoint to the tail of the donkey doing much the same thing.

Then there was the thin shriek of a horn and a cry of alarm. "Robbers!" one of the men shouted, pointing first one direction then another at two masses of men swarming through the scrub towards them, their own wild yelling now adding to the cacophony of men, animals and horn.

Yehuda had only been with the caravan for a few weeks and was not yet trusted with a blade: it was not unknown for robbers to insinuate their own assassins into plum but well-guarded targets. But he knew what to do. Like the few other unarmed men, he grabbed as many rocks as he could and scurried to find what shelter was to be found; his task would be to cause as much havoc amongst the attackers as he could—and hope that the attack was over before those attackers decided to remove his annoying and poorly defended presence from the fray.

Unfortunately for the caravan this time the attackers at least matched the defenders, even with one of them being a man on a horse. While the mass of them kept the other men occupied, three surrounded Ananias, preventing him from riding the others down and threatening to drag him from his horse. They were nimble enough of foot to avoid being struck by horse or rider; neither they nor Ananias wanted the horse itself damaged, but Ananias knew they would value it less than he did, so a note of desperation entered his eyes.

Yehuda saw none of that, only the narrow focus of his own concerns. One of the robbers had just kicked a defender, who had fallen back and hit his head on the ground, when Yehuda's rock hit him on the shoulder. The man snarled, quickly decided that he could dispatch his new attacker in time to get back and finish off the old, and ran yelling toward him. Yehuda was fast; this time, he was also lucky. One stone found the man's arm, enough to make him turn his head; the next struck him hard in the temple and he fell merely an arm's length from Yehuda.

Yehuda looked around, adrenalin fueling his battle rage and accelerating his native speed. He saw the knots of battling men; the desperate straits of Ananias; the short sword just beyond the insensate fingers of the man he had felled: and knew what had to be done. He reached out, took the sword, and ran.

Some instinct kept him silent. He did not charge into the fray yelling a battle cry. Instead he ran silent and low, dodging through the scrub. There was a man just ahead now, his back toward Yehuda, reaching for the horse's reins with one hand while waving a sword toward Ananias with the other. Yehuda was not a trained warrior. He did not know how best to plunge a blade, let alone how to defend himself. One of the other attackers noticed him and began to yell a warning. Before the man could turn and no doubt make short work of him, Yehuda swung his weapon in a low arc across the back of his target's legs; the man fell with a scream, his hamstrings cut.

Then it was over. With only two tormentors Ananias cut one down, then the other backed away and ran. Pounding hooves alerted their fellows, who glanced aside to see a fury descending upon them from on high. Then they too ran.

Ananias chased them a few steps but prudently chose not to pursue them. He wheeled his mount, trotted back and surveyed the scene grimly. The only robber remaining not dead or unconscious was the man Yehuda had felled from behind. Ananias glared down on him, then dismounted, marching over to him, sword held out before him. He lifted the man's chin with his sword, examining him sourly. He was old, possibly even forty years of age, with a grim hard visage reflecting his chosen profession and numerous scars testifying to its dangers. The quality of his clothing and sword indicated he might even be the bandit chieftain.

"You! What is your name?"

The man just spat on the ground, and Ananias pushed his sword harder against his throat. "Your name, Bandit?"

"Bandit? Traitor!"

"I? I am a simple merchant, no traitor. And you are a robber, no patriot."

"You enrich yourself at others' expense, helping pay for the Roman dogs who have taken our Kingdom!"

"People must live, robber. I buy honest goods with honest coin, and bring it to those who need it most. It is enough that the Romans rule us. Should we stop living as well?"

"Yes, you and your dogs go on living your fat lives while the Romans rape us. Where is your courage? If the people would rise up, they would throw off their shackles and return to the ways of the Lord!

But the people choose to go on as if it does not matter that Rome desecrates our Temple and eats the fat of the land. You help them in their blindness, you bring them their comforts and their wealth! Do not condemn me, traitor. Look to yourself, and weep for Israel. Weep for the Israel you have made and betrayed!"

"You speak fine words, Bandit. But they are pretty words to hide from yourself the men you kill, the children you leave fatherless, the widows you leave destitute: for what? Do you think some bandits in the wilderness stealing the effort of others will throw off the might of Rome? You will achieve only your deaths, in addition to all the others."

"Then at least I die trying, not as a lapdog licking the boots of its conquerors, that they might throw it a bone or two!"

Ananias pushed his sword harder. "So you say. Repent now, before the Lord High God. That will not save you from justice on Earth. But perhaps it will redeem you and your children in the eyes of our Lord."

"I have nothing to repent of, Traitor. It is you who should repent, and join me."

"I have said I am no traitor. I too await the Messiah who will bring us back to God and liberate our land from the oppressors. I shall know that Messiah when I see him, for shall not the mark of God be upon him?"

He looked sourly at the man. "And that Messiah is not you, Robber. So your name, hero? You care for no man but yourself. But perhaps you care for your sons. Tell me your name, that your sons may know of your fate."

The man spat, but relented. "I am Abbas. And my name will be known long after yours is forgotten."

Ananias nodded, and lowered his sword. Then in one stroke he slashed it across Abbas' throat, and the man fell forward into the sand, his lifeblood pulsing out and staining it deep red.

"Nail him to a tree! And the others!"

This act did not shock the others. The penalty for robbery was death. They could spend their own money treating, feeding and guarding such prisoners; spending their wealth to keep them alive at risk of them escaping or being freed and wreaking their own rough vengeance; but the end would be the same. The wilderness had its own rules and justice.

Their dead they buried. Their wounded they bound as best they could and if they could not walk, strapped them to the backs of beasts.

Then they departed, continuing along their way.

Behind them, three bodies hung nailed from trees along the way as a warning to other robbers of the fate that may await them. Above the body hanging in the center of the tableau, his head hanging down and his beard matted and stained red with blood, was a crude sign with rough letters drawn in pitch:

Abbas
King of the Robbers

~~~

That night around the campfire Ananias came up to Yehuda.

"You fought well today. Had you not, mayhap none of us would be alive to speak of it. Take this, you have earned it."

Then he unwrapped a blade and presented it to Yehuda, supported flat on his two palms. It was a curved sword, a *sicara;* longer than most and more like a short sword than a dagger, but still of that type. But the quality of its iron and decorations spoke of an origin far from here in the fabulous East, and Yehuda wondered what trail of trade and robbery had brought it from its homeland into the possession of Abbas and now on to him. He turned it in the light, admiring its deadly beauty.

"I thank you, Ananias. My arm is your arm; my sword is your sword."

"Yes, yes," replied Ananias with mock asperity, "that is all very well. But now who will collect the dung?"

Chapter 4: Clay and Flesh

Life in a caravan was hard, but not without its pleasures. A man of his means could not hope to own many of the goods they traded; but a man of his profession could see, touch and handle them; even acquire damaged or offcut portions for this own, or taste rare spices and wines. Many of his countrymen rarely left the town of their birth, and if they did it was a rare, long and dangerous journey: he remembered his own youthful adventure to Jerusalem. Such brief and fraught journeys were as likely to confirm the travelers in the unique virtues of their hometown as broaden their minds to the virtues of others. But Yehuda visited villages, towns and cities the length and breadth of the country. His master did not venture far from the lands of Israel, rarely travelling beyond Damascus; but if Yehuda did not grow into a man of the world, at least he grew into a man of his part of it; and if he did not visit far lands, still he came to know many of their natives, traders like themselves only more adventurous or brave. As an inoculation against provincial narrow-mindedness, such experience was unparalleled.

Yehuda had not yet married. He had little money for a dowry, and as one undistinguished son among many his family could be called upon for little more. Plus his itinerant lifestyle was not attractive to potential wives nor indeed to himself, as most of the advantages of marriage would be foregone much of the time. He had the same lusts as any other man his age but these he happily satisfied with the harlots of the towns they passed through. Though the stricter priests and mystics might frown upon such means of relief, and righteous citizens might look down on such women with contempt, Yehuda did not care. The women were tolerated; whatever the public attitude to them, still they managed enough custom to bring bread to their tables and kohl to their eyes. If it was a sin it was an accepted one.

Sin or not, it was an activity shared by other men of the caravan: all the unmarried ones and many of the married ones. Yehuda felt a casual contempt for the women he bedded, but it was more a contempt absorbed from his culture than anything deeply held within his own soul. If he cared to examine it, it vanished like the morning mist when seen by the sun. They did him a service that he enjoyed immensely; they did it without censure and indeed with eagerness; and if some or all of the eagerness was not entirely sincere, the pleasure they sold was real.

So if he had been asked, Yehuda would not have said his life was more or less than he had expected. He just lived it, following it where it took him and doing the best he could with the hand God or Fate had dealt him: working hard, following his God and taking what pleasures life could provide to ease its burdens.

He stayed with the caravan for six years. Then some minor cut on his leg became inflamed; the inflammation became a suppurating wound; the suppuration hit his bloodstream and became a raging fever. The caravan could not care for him, carry him or wait for him to live or die. So he was simply left.

They found a widow who was glad for the money to take care of the dying stranger. Yehuda had accumulated a purse of coin over his years; Ananias added some more. It would be enough for some months, or some lesser time and a funeral. If against the odds Yehuda recovered quickly, he could perhaps catch up with the caravan or meet it at one of its expected stops. Beyond that he was on his own.

The widow did her duty. She was old, embittered by aged grief and long poverty, wondering why her God had abandoned her. She knew the story of Job and it gave her comfort: though she could not have said whether the comfort came from its tale of final redemption or the picture of someone whose suffering exceeded her own. But she fed, cooled and cleaned the man given into her care. If he died, she could keep the remainder of the money; if he lived, and feared God, he might be generous and ease her life even more. She dreaded an illness that would outlive his funds: but she could not believe that God would add that burden to her life on top of the rest. Perhaps if she had studied

17

Job more carefully she would have been more worried.

However Yehuda was young and strong, and after a week of desperate clinging to life his fever broke. But even after he could walk and take care of himself he was still weak, and it would be some time before he would be able to travel any distance, especially any distance through the inhospitable wilderness. He counted his funds and the days ahead of him, and knew he would have to find employment.

It was difficult at first. There were always those seeking day laborers, but there were always men looking for just such work. The times were few when the weakened Yehuda was chosen, whether because the others had already been taken or he managed to look stronger than he was. Perhaps if had been chosen more often he would have become equal to the tasks quicker: but if any of his prospective hirers even thought in those terms, none would have been interested in building him up to some future employer's benefit.

One of his jobs entailed driving an ox cart laden with bricks to a building site. After offloading, the builder told him to wait while he checked whether any materials could be returned with the cart, and he fell to chatting with an old potter while he rested in the shade. The potter complained that his apprentice, on whom the potter had lavished more care than any other mortal master would have, had died. The old man was now left without an assistant, and who amongst the lazy youth of today was interested in learning a trade? How could his business sustain him in his declining years, when his body no longer had its youthful strength?

Yehuda asked to inspect the man's product. It was well made but simple. *So much in life must be paid for in blood. If the Lord offers you a gift, take it with both hands.*

"Teach me, and I shall become your assistant," he offered.

The potter stopped in mid-rant to stare at him, surprised. Apprentices were usually taken as boys, not men already set in their skills and opinions. But he narrowed his eyes shrewdly.

"You are too old."

"I am not so old I cannot learn."

"I cannot pay much."

"My needs are small."

"You will be useless."

"You will have my arms to do your carrying, my legs to do your traveling, and my strength to help you in all else. All I ask in return is the coin to live and the training to help you even more, and perhaps one day to carry on your work. Pay me but two denarii a day for two weeks. If by the end of that time I am useless, dismiss me. If I am not, pay me what I am worth to you."

"Two denarii!? What am I, King Solomon!? A half, no more."

"The laborers in the field receive one. Do you expect any work out of me, while I starve? One."

The potter sighed dramatically. "You take advantage of a poor old man, knowing he is at your mercy. Very well, one. After that, we shall see. I am Matthias, son of Shimon. Be here tomorrow an hour past sunrise."

~~~

Yehuda had an affinity for clay. In the battle with Abbas he had seen the patterns of the fight and knew where to strike the needed blow. That same inner sight he now applied to the potter's art: he had an understanding of form and how to make it rise from the formless mud of the clay he worked.

His native talent was visible to the old potter from early on, but talent was never enough: skill took practice. Matthias did not let him work with the finest clay or on the finest jobs; he worked with the gritty, low-quality clays. The poor who were content with that were usually content with the poorer shapes that often arose from Yehuda's hands; if Matthias did not see spectacular returns from what he viewed as his overly generous investment in his new pupil, at least it was worth his while to continue the arrangement.

Thus did Yehuda's skill increase, until finally Matthias felt comfortable in diverting all but the most demanding jobs to his understudy and companion. Yehuda had long since left the old widow and moved in with his new master.

Then one day Yehuda arose from his bed, and when he called for Matthias there was no answer. He had died during the night. He had not been ill and nor had he been ancient, merely old. He had just died, as men sometimes do.

The remaining sons of Matthias had no skill nor interest in the potter's art. The eldest, who had, had died many years ago; hence the apprentice Yehuda had replaced. After Matthias had been laid in his tomb the sons came to Yehuda to discuss the fate of their father's goods. They could sell the house and the pots, but to get any good price for the latter would take time, and a man would have to remain there to do it. Many of the pots had been made by Yehuda, and he could lay claim to a portion. Yehuda pointed out that if the business remained running they would receive an ongoing income, likely to greatly exceed the immediate benefit of selling. Finally it was agreed: Yehuda would remain as sole operator of the pottery business. He would pay the brothers rent on the dwelling, which was also the workshop and stall; he would pay them four fifths of the sale price of the existing pots and a tithe of any new ones.

And so Yehuda came to be a potter under his own direction. His affinity for the clay under his hands fused with his growing skill in forming it to match his vision, and his reputation in the town grew.

One day an important man of the town, a Jew but one who had long since seen the direction of the winds and affected Roman airs, summoned Yehuda into his presence. As Yehuda entered his home guided by a servant, he could not help admiring the handsome black and white mosaic decorating the entranceway floor, a sign of his host's wealth and political leaning.

The man beckoned to him to sit.

"So, Yehuda of Kerioth, I have heard good words of your work and my own eyes agree. I should like to give my wife a gift of fine pottery. I am Lucius."

"Lucius? Is that not a Roman name? Are you not a Jew?"

Lucius shrugged. "Jew I am, indeed. Do not think I forget my heritage. But was the Kingdom of David unchanged from the herders of goats the Lord chose the Patriarchs from? Are we unchanged from that Kingdom? The wise man knows when the times have changed, and sets his sails accordingly."

"I met a man once who would have killed you for those words."

"Perhaps he is not alone. What became of him?"

"He is dead."

"Well there you are. Life is dangerous. The man who would kill me for making accommodation with the men of Rome has returned to dust and ashes, while I who chose the other path yet breathe. Either the Lord Most High approves of my course, or his ways are too mysterious for we mortals to divine them from our fates, and we must follow our own wisdom."

Yehuda shrugged. "Perhaps. We must all choose our paths. Certainly there are some who would say that any who do not fight the Romans support them; in that I am no better than you. Perhaps they are right, perhaps not."

"Well then! If you have chosen to support the Romans, maybe you too need to know your Roman name. Do you know what it is?"

"No."

"Let me see... they do insist on hammering our musical syllables into their own barbaric tongue"—he looked around in mock nervousness, as if worried that some Roman might overhear him describing them as 'barbarians'. "Yes... also Greek, if I am not mistaken. So yes. 'Judas', they would call you 'Judas'."

"I think I shall prefer to be known forever as Yehuda."

"As you wish. So to business. Will you take my commission?"

"I am always willing to speak. What is this commission?"

"Observe this amphora," the man said, pointing to a handsome urn by the wall. "Observe the quality and color of the clay, the fineness of the design. Observe how well it fits the niche it sits in, as if the niche were built for the urn, not the urn placed in the niche. Now observe the five empty niches in this room. I should like them filled with something similar. The same size, the same quality, but with variations on the theme. Can you do it?"

Yehuda walked over and examined it carefully. "I know where clay like this may be found. But it is some journey away, and not all fine. It will be expensive to acquire the quantity. And as you say, the pots are large and the quality high."

The man nodded, but pointed out the risk to himself if Yehuda's work was not as good as promised, and the benefit to Yehuda if his finest work were to be displayed in the house of a leading citizen. Yehuda remarked that a man should not stint in a gift to his wife, especially if his wife came from a wealthy family. This haggling went on for some time, until finally the men agreed on a figure.

Yehuda sketched the amphora and returned to his workshop. There he designed another five amphorae to match its form and decoration with none being the same. Like a family of brothers, who might look the same to a stranger but their mother would know each one. He took his designs to Lucius, who expressed his delight.

"Excellent! If you can make them as well as you can sketch them, you will be worth the gold you extorted from me!"

~~~

Yehuda had not lied about the clay. He hired a man with an ox cart and a pair of shovels, and they headed out of town along a rutted track into the wilderness. Enough rain fell here for there to be water under the ground and seams of clay, moist enough to work and firm enough to hold. Matthias had gained deep knowledge over his long career and passed it on to Yehuda. There was an extensive run of the particular type of clay Yehuda needed in one of the arroyos, much of it contaminated with pieces of rock but with large patches of fine, pure material.

As they passed through a small canyon, Yehuda felt someone's eyes on him and looked around nervously. Two men and an ox cart were not a notably tempting target for robbers but nor were they immune, and Yehuda made sure his *sicara* was loose and within easy reach.

Then he saw him. A man stood on a cliff, watching them. He was swathed in a dark, ragged material, pieces of it whipping in the wind, a part wrapped around his face to protect him from the dust blown on that wind. He just stood watching them with a strange intensity, and Yehuda relaxed. It was not unknown for ascetics and mystics to wander in the wilderness, some for years, though how they survived in this unpromising land Yehuda could not imagine. Perhaps it was true that God looked after his own. And this man would be one of them.

Yehuda could not truly see his face, but there was something about the man's eyes that sent a shiver down his spine: though whether a shiver from his past or his future he could not tell. He stood there for some minutes, staring up at the stranger, wondering. Then he flicked his finger in signal to his companion, and they continued along their way.

The man on the cliff stayed watching them, immobile, until they had vanished into the wilderness.

~~~

Yehuda brought his cart of fine clay back to his workshop. As they passed again through the canyon he had looked up, wondering if the watcher on the cliff would still be there. But the cliff was empty, with nothing but the sky to observe their passing.

Under his hands the amphorae rose from the clay even as he had drawn them. The clay was fine and without flaw: none of the pots cracked in the firing, as some could do. He brought them to Lucius, who clapped his hands in approval at the sight of them.

"Excellent indeed! Yes, Judas, a prize. My wife will be most pleased!"

And so she was. In their bed she gave him the rewards a husband could hope for from such a gift; among her family she trilled of what a fine husband she had. And so Lucius gained not only pleasure in his home but the approval of his wife's wealthy family. Both he and Yehuda were happy.

~~~

Yehuda stood at his stall, calling out for business from the passersby. There was a temporary lull and he leant back against the wall. He reached into the pouch at his waste and pulled out a fig, took a bite and chewed reflectively.

A woman caught his eye. She was modestly attired, with a long black dress and a veil covering the lower half of her face, like many other women. She was young, probably not having seen twenty years. He could not have said what about her held his attention. Yes, she was attractive; but not exceptionally so, no more than many others. Yes, she had that female walk, her hips swinging more than a man's: the kind of walk that harlots on the prowl accentuated as part of their signaling, like their padded breasts and darkened eyes. But this woman was not doing that, just walking as a woman walked. Perhaps it was the way she held her head; perhaps in some way he was seeing the totality of her being.

All he knew was that he liked to watch her walk by. A stranger might have thought his gaze improper, but no more than the standard lusts of disreputable merchants. He might have thought it himself. But his soul was held more than his eyes.

He did not think the woman had noticed him or his gaze, intent as she was on her own destination. But as she walked away down the street she turned to look directly at him. Noticing the direction of his gaze her eyes flashed, but he imagined that beneath her veil he saw the start of a smile. Then she tossed her head haughtily and continued on whatever mission had brought her past his stall.

But it seemed to him that her hips swung somewhat more than they had before.

CHAPTER 5: A GIRL'S LIFE

As in much of the world of that time, if one could choose one's sex it would be male. The lot of women was not to be envied: it was men who ruled and decided, women who meekly obeyed.

Perhaps not always meekly, and many a man may have paid for his privileges through that lamentable lack. But still, many avenues a man regarded as his right were denied to women, whether by law, by custom or simply by lack of suitable education.

Yet daughters were often named after famous women, as if their parents wished the shine of that fame to reflect upon the child even as the parents did their best to limit their daughter's chance of any fame of her own. As is true around the world, parents love their children even if they cannot see beyond the strictures of their own culture; even if when viewed objectively, or perhaps merely from the perspective of history, they treat them poorly.

The turbulence of Israel's history did not begin with the Romans. Since its beginning the land had seen victories and defeats, the rise of kings and the slaughter of their sons. Had not the Promised Land been attained in the first place by the defeat of its Canaanite inhabitants? No doubt that was not the first such event, but whatever triumphs and defeats had shaped the Canaanites themselves were long lost to the memory of men.

Centuries ago the legendary Alexander the Great had burned like a meteor through history. Empires that in their day had played their own part in Israel's tribulations fell before his march: the mighty Persia; ancient Egypt; fabulous Babylon and the lands of the Assyrians. But like a meteor he had flamed and vanished: he had died young, conquering the world but never ruling it.

His generals divided Alexander's legacy among them. First Israel was ruled by the Ptolemaic Kingdom; then by the Seleucid Empire.

Then in Israel's last days of glory another Yehuda, known as HaMakabi, defeated the empire which had sacked Jerusalem and attempted to suppress the Jewish God. Ironically, his victory was assisted by the weakening of the Seleucids by the very Romans who later imposed their own rule. Yehuda's brother set up a Jewish dynasty to rule Judea and its surrounding regions. This Hasmonean dynasty lasted mere decades before finally being crushed by Rome, who installed Herod the Great as their client king. Seeking legitimacy from within as well as without, Herod married a Hasmonean princess renowned for her beauty. Unfortunately neither her beauty, her lineage nor Herod's desire to join himself to that lineage granted her a long and happy life. Eight years and four children after their marriage she was executed for treason. Perhaps Herod's grief was genuine; or perhaps his fear of his rivals was greater than his love for her. In any case, all of the most renowned of her family met similar fates.

The princess's name was Miriam. By the time Yehuda of Kerioth was born, more than a quarter of Judean women shared her name.

One of those women lived in a small town in Galilee and married a carpenter named Yossef; the first of their children, born perhaps a little too soon after their wedding night, they named Yeshua. Another, born some years after that to a blacksmith in a different town of Galilee, would intersect Yehuda's life via quite a different path.

~~~

Abichail was a strict man. He was proud of his sons and loved his daughters according to his lights. Those daughters might have described those lights as dim, had they known another perspective from which to judge them. As it was they lived the life given them without judging it; in their worst moments they may have prayed to their God for something better, but they lived meekly and dutifully as was their lot, or at least as they had to if they wanted to avoid a beating.

He was a blacksmith, strong of arm and short of temper. His skill at his craft he had learned from his father, then exceeded; he was now a wealthy man. He despised the Romans and hated sinners. He had a lawyer's attention for the rules of his religion, especially as they pertained to the rights and privileges of fathers, husbands and men; his attention to the privileges granted to others was rather less focused. After all, he judged if he ever cared to consider the issue, if others thought he owed them something let them be men and claim it. It certainly did not occur to him that a mere female was in no such position.

Abichail's wealth did not fully satisfy him. There were always others with larger houses, more gold or finer raiment. To his credit he did not grumble about this, merely worked his hardest. But he was proud when his sons became men about town themselves and could give him the gifts due their patriarch. Daughters could not help him in that way. They were good for little: they helped where their feeble arms and feebler intellects allowed; they served him food and wine; and above all, he looked forward to the day when he could marry them off for a handsome dowry.

All the daughters knew that their lot was to be given in marriage as soon as they were of age, soon after their twelfth year. They knew something of the rites of marriage; something of the needs of men; something of the pain and risks of childbirth. They looked forward to their adult lives with a mixture of trepidation of the unknown and anticipation of the new. If they were lucky their husband would be handsome and kind; if they were very lucky their conjoining might one day grow into love. They did not need luck for him to be rich: if he were not, he could not afford the dowry their father would demand.

Miriam was not the eldest daughter, hence not the first to wed. The eldest could have married better, could have married worse. In a bad mood she would tell her sisters of her husband's boorish nature, his temper, his demands. In a brighter mood she would speak of the times of contented companionship, and whisper of the startling joys of the marital bed.

When Miriam was twelve she was betrothed to one of her father's friends, Binyamin son of Yohanan. He was an older man, even older than her own father; a widower seeking the help and comfort of a new wife in his declining years. Miriam looked upon him with disfavor: he was neither handsome nor showing promise of kindness; the way he looked at her spoke of the desire to possess and rule as by his right. For it was not ready wit or mirthful company that drew Binyamin and Abichail together; indeed, such qualities were of little interest to her father. They were friends because they shared the strictness of their faith, and enjoyed bemoaning the inferior virtues of those less ritually perfect or more kindly disposed to human frailty.

By the rules of their religion Miriam had to agree to the marriage; by the customs of her people, let alone the face of her father, such agreement was a formality. She would need a very strong reason to deny the match; mere dislike was not considered a reason at all. So she looked at him when the question was asked, and assented.

And so Miriam was married, not long before her thirteenth year began. Her proofs of virginity were clear and the marriage was not only consummated but blessed. And so Abichail happily received his dowry, Binyamin happily took his wife, and Miriam, the least important part of the equation, took on the duties of wife.

Miriam would not have said she was happy but nor would she say she was unhappy. Life with Binyamin was much like life with her father, except that she shared his bed. She had hoped that might pay for the rest; that in the Lord's great wisdom the responsibilities and duties of being a woman, wife and mother would be matched by the pleasures inherent in those roles. But she was disappointed. In bed her husband cared only for his pleasure; that might not have mattered, except that he was rough and fast in reaching the gasping and heaving that she imagined meant the peak of his own joy, and she knew meant the planting of his seed in her body. It was not that there was no pleasure; sometimes she yearned for his hands and lips on the secret parts of her body; for the rubbing and thrusting, and the scintillation it spread along her nerves; but any promise it held was like the light of a dawn in which the sun never rose. She wondered how her eldest sister was so easily pleased by the process.

The seeds he planted never sprouted. He had not had children by his first two wives, for which he had grown to despise them. Perhaps Miriam too was barren. But he did not have time to grow to despise her, for after only two years of marriage he took the fever. Miriam cared for him as best she could, but he did not see another Sabbath.

He was wealthy enough to have a number of mourners, who wailed and rent their robes and scattered ashes on their heads as he was laid to rest in his tomb. Miriam looked on, sad at the passing of any human being—if he had not been the best husband, nor had he been intentionally cruel—but finding that the grief displayed so professionally by the mourners found no answer from her own soul.

Merely theoretical visitors while he was alive, Binyamin's relatives proved their actual existence by turning up along with skillfully portrayed grief upon his death. Women did not inherit from their husbands, being entitled only to whatever goods were theirs including any gifts or bequests from their husbands. So Binyamin's estates and possessions would go to his relatives not to Miriam.

However her father had negotiated a very favorable *ketubbah* regarding what Miriam would receive if her husband died. He had done this out of simple and habitual greed to get the best price possible for his daughter, coupled with the consideration of how much older Binyamin was than her. He cared nothing for that age difference in any calculation of his daughter's happiness, but it loomed large in calculations relating to his own future benefit. For Binyamin's part, having outlived two wives it never occurred to him that he would not outlive the third; or perhaps he merely wished to reduce the amount his relatives received if he failed to. In his view they were all sinners and scoundrels, far from reaching the heights of virtue he himself inhabited, indeed not even trying. Any discomfort he might have felt at neglecting the rights of his relatives was negated by the comfort of acting virtuously toward his wife. For did not the scriptures speak of the virtues of looking after the widow and orphan? If he did not think often of his wife's happiness when he was alive, at least he supported her according to his duty. It was even easier to support her when he was dead and it cost him nothing, especially if that meant less for his worthless relatives.

For all his faults, Binyamin recognized that his wife was a virtuous woman. Perhaps he even loved her.

Or perhaps not.

Neither Miriam nor her father saw any advantage in her remaining at Binyamin's house. It was too large for her alone and the automatic rights of widows extended only to what living space they personally required; living there in the presence of Binyamin's disreputable relatives or likely even less reputable tenants was unappetizing and, in Abichail's view, bad for her virtue. So Miriam moved back into her father's house.

She saw her younger sister wed, giving her advice in some ways better and some ways worse than their oldest sister had imparted. But she did not wed again herself. She was now at an age at which her father could not force her to marry. He frequently encouraged her to do so; occasionally raged at her to do so, for he thought a single woman was against God's will and a temptation to men to sin. But rage as he would, she just looked at him calmly.

"Father, I honor you as is my duty. But the choice to marry or not is mine. I will marry according to my own choice, when I choose."

"Oh, woe is me, to have such a disobedient daughter!"

"I obey you in all things, where God demands obedience. God does not demand obedience in this. Would you put yourself above God?"

"Insolent girl! Why do I feed you, when you speak to me thus?!"

"Father. If you no longer love me as your daughter, do you cast me out? You are master of your household. Say the word and I shall depart. With my *ketubbah*, as is my right. But I beg you, father. Do you not wish me to stay, to serve you as I did as a girl? To use my *ketubbah* not only for my own comfort but for yours? My *ketubbah* is sufficient for my needs. But I would be alone. Men would—look at me. I wish only to remain a virtuous daughter. Please, father, let me remain under your protection. One day I will marry again. It is just that the day has not yet come."

"Well! Let it not be said that Abichail son of Miykah would cast his own daughter out of his house! But mind your virtue, woman! Now fetch me wine!"

In truth Miriam had no intention of marrying. Perhaps one day she would if circumstance demanded. But for now her life was comfortable, and though her father was domineering she retained more freedom than she had as unripe girl or owned wife. Perhaps not in law, but in her ability to leave without destitution and the fact that her father was better off with her here than gone. Women had little power in this society. But that made them experts in using what power they had.

~~~

So Miriam's life went on, day succeeding day as it had always. She lived with her father, sharing his meals, his successes and his failures; his dutiful daughter except in the one point of her refusal to marry. Her mother died, succumbing to some disease of the lungs which made her breathing painful, her coughs even more so; until the night when Miriam was soothing her brow with a wet rag then waited for the next ragged breath, a breath which never came.

Miriam had loved her mother. Like most young girls whose lives had been spared tragedy she had been a vivacious, laughing child. But the years had worn her down, and by the time Miriam could speak to her as a fellow woman not her godlike mother she was faded and fatalistic. Her favorite answer to any question was, "It is as the Lord wills." But she loved her sons and her daughters with a love less strict and more understanding than that of her husband. If anything she loved her daughters more, for she felt her sons needed it less, being born with so much more. When Miriam had returned she had been sorry for her loss but glad for her company; when Miriam had described her marriage, even its most intimate details, she had nodded in understanding. Then she had taken Miriam's hand.

"It is as the Lord wills, daughter. As are all things, from the rise of kings to the fall of a bird. I wished for a happier life for you, my babe who suckled at my breast, my daughter who played in the rain, my beloved Miriam who gained then lost a husband. And I believe you will have it. I do not know why, but I know that the future holds something for you: something great. It may be tragic, but if so the greatness will exceed the tragedy. And at the end of your life you will look back on it, and be glad for every minute you lived. And I will look up from Sheol, if I am granted such vision, and be glad for all of your life, and all of mine."

As much as her father desired her to marry, her mother understood her refusal. And while she did not dare oppose her husband in his presence, she gave Miriam the fuel of understanding and acceptance in his absence.

But now she was dead, and Miriam and her father were the only remaining inhabitants of the family home. The two sons still worked in the smithy, having learnt their trade from their father and, finding their own affinity for it, continued in the family trade. But they were married with their own households, and were only present for work or the occasional family gatherings.

Being wealthy they had their own house, built around a courtyard with four small rooms on the upper story for sleeping in the relative cool of the evening. Once she had shared one of these rooms with her sisters; another had been shared by her brothers; while the third was her parents' bedchamber. The fourth had always been a store room where guests could bed down if needed; on their departure the brothers' room had become its twin.

So now her and her father's rooms with their single occupants faced each other across the courtyard. Curtains could be drawn across their entrances for necessary modesty.

With his wife's death Abichail did not become more mellow. It may have been the shock of losing the wife he loved, or at least was useful to him; it may have been the loss of the wife who shared his bed and brought him the intimate comforts that came with that. The needs that comfort fulfilled he refused to assuage by the other means which might have been available to him; or if he did, their sinfulness merely amplified his bitterness. He became more dedicated in his pursuit of ritualistic perfection; more strident in his condemnation of the sins of the flesh.

More afraid that his daughter's refusal to marry any of the excellent old men he brought her way was a sign of an adulterous heart, of sins not to be suspected or named.

CHAPTER 6: TEMPTATION

One day Miriam was on an errand. In the future she would look back on that day and have no memory of her purpose that morning. She would only remember one scene, one moment in the long reel of her life on which the sun, or the eye of God, shone, casting it in harsh relief and consigning all else to darkness.

She was walking up the street. Though she could not remember her errand she could remember the sound of her sandals slapping against the ground, the feel of her robe blowing against her skin, and the hot, dusty smell of the air.

She was innocently going about her business, her mind on the mundane needs of thread for sewing or grain, or even eggs, for eating: far from questions of passion or destiny. It was not until she had walked past him that her awareness caught up with what her eye had seen: a man, unremarkable in every way, bar that he was looking at her.

Her mind held the image, though she did not know why. He was lean, hard of muscle, yet relaxed in posture; just a man, chewing on a fig. But there was something about his eyes. She knew lust; she had seen it in the eyes of her husband as he pulled the robe from her shoulders; she had seen it in the eyes of strangers who had caught a chance glimpse of ankle or more intimate flesh, or merely her form under her clothes: their own imagination doing the rest. But the look in his eyes wasn't that. Or it included that, while transcending it; as if his lust was more than for her flesh, but for her spirit.

I have been in the sun too long, she thought. *I must be about to faint, if I am having imaginings such as these.*

She turned to look, expecting to see just a man, expecting the mirage of her fevered imagination to be exposed for the tawdry reality it was. And so it was: he was still there, still chewing his fig, his strangely intense stare still directed at her—or at the part of her below her waist. Her eyes flashed in anger at his impertinence, that he would dare stare at a respectable widow in such a manner; but something about that stare made her lips move upward in contradiction to her contempt.

She tossed her head in denial and refusal, and continued along the street as if his existence were unworthy of notice. *Men! You cannot look at a woman's face, because all you care for from us is what we can draw forth from below your own waists! Well, Potter, stare as you will. You will never see me again, let alone discover the hidden secrets you imagine.*

But she wondered at the tingling she now felt in her own loins. She was surprised that she would feel it now. Men did not interest her; whatever promises that tingling held she knew were the promises of liars: sweet of tongue but bringing naught but the desolation of betrayal.

But the look in his eyes stayed with her; and whenever she cared to remember those eyes, the lying tingling returned.

~~~

Two weeks later, Miriam was taking breakfast with her father. The previous evening he had been invited to the home of one of his customers, an important man of the town, to discuss some ironwork the man wanted. While there, being served olives and wine—a proof of Abichail's own standing in the town!—the man had proudly pointed out some urns he had recently acquired for his wife. Abichail had decided he should have one of like quality; not as ostentatious, for that was unseemly, but equally elegant, befitting the family's honor and position.

To his annoyance, Abichail had turned his ankle on his way home and it was still painful to walk, but he was keen to pursue this new acquisition without delay. While normally he would deal with such matters himself, Miriam was used to performing simple purchases and errands around the town. A mere potter was really no different from a lentil or olive merchant; even a woman could convey Abichail's requirement and price to one. If the man wished to question or quibble, well then, he could come to Abichail to discuss it.

"Here, daughter. I have written out what I want, along with Lucius' words of recommendation—that he may know he deals with a man of importance!—and my price. You need do nothing except show him this and return his reply. Will you do this for your poor father, daughter?"

"I can do that, father. Where is this potter?"

"It is a man named Judas, of Kerioth. His workshop lies in the street leading west from the synagogue. You know it?"

Miriam's breath caught in her throat. But on what grounds could she refuse? That the man had looked upon her with lust in his eyes? That her own flesh had answered with its own lust? That she still saw his eyes when she closed hers for sleep?

No. She would face the man, if indeed it were the same man, as he deserved. Her eyes would be iron and her voice stone. She would deliver her father's message and return his reply. She would give him no acknowledgement: not of the past, nor of his manhood, nor of the future. He would learn that his damnable eyes meant nothing to her. And she could forget him.

It never occurred to her that he might already have forgotten her.

"Yes, father, I know it. It shall be done. A daughter of Abichail does not fear potters."

~~~

For the second time in recent memory she walked up that street, this time acutely aware of pots. She was not sure whether it was regret or anticipation which leapt to her throat as she approached the first potter she saw. It was the man.

This was not a busy time of the day and he was working on the decoration of a pot, his back to her.

"Are you Judas, of Kerioth?"

He spun around, startled that a woman would speak to him in such a peremptory fashion.

"I am."

He stared at her for a few moments. "You! I mean, who are you?"

"I am Miriam, daughter of Abichail, widow of Binyamin. Why do you look at me so, insolent man? I am an honest widow, not to be stared at by rough tradesmen."

"You are not a Roman. Why do you address me as one? My name is Yehuda."

"Your pardon, Yehuda. That is the name I was given."

I will forgive you anything, so long as you stay.

"What brings you here, honest widow?"

"My father wishes to offer you a commission," she replied, holding forth her father's offer.

Yehuda took it and examined it. "Ah, yes, the esteemed Lucius. I see. I can do it, but your father's offer is low. You are bold, for an honest widow. Does your father wish you to haggle on his behalf?"

"He thinks it a fair price and expects you to accept it. He is unable to walk at present. If you want the commission but wish to haggle you must visit him yourself to do so. If not, not. It is nothing to me."

"Nothing?" he said softly, giving her the stare she remembered, desired, and feared.

"Perhaps I should not wish you to do so. You frighten me. I do not want you to know where I live."

"Why do I frighten you?"

"You stare at me like a madman."

"Is that what you see? Madness?"

"If it is not madness, then it is worse."

"I am sure you are an honest widow, for I have seen you before. But you are more than that, or we would not be having a conversation of this nature. Instead you would run to your father and tell him I refused his commission, or have him set his sons to beat me. You want something from me. Perhaps something I am willing to give."

"No, I think I shall have my father beat you for your insolence."

"Go then, Miriam, daughter of Abichail."

Her eyes flashed as they had on that day a fortnight ago, but now he saw her cheeks redden. She turned abruptly to go, then stopped.

Slowly she turned back to face him. She noticed that his unholy eyes had not descended this time, but remained looking directly at her, waiting to meet her gaze. Yet the tingling in her loins was the greater for it.

"I... I do not wish to go, just yet. Our business is not yet concluded and I... would be... would be failing in my duty to my father... if I did not bring him a firm answer, for his heart is set on your handiwork."

"Will you have me beaten, after that?"

"I... I should, insolent man! But your wife might not forgive me if I caused that face to become even uglier."

"I have no wife."

"No... wife? I see. Forgive me again, Yehuda of Kerioth."

She shook herself. "And stop staring at me. Do you accept my father's offer, or not?"

He smiled. "His offer is too low. If he wants the pots, he must go higher." He sighed. "Thus I must visit him. Will you lead me there, woman?"

"I will not have one such as you follow me through the streets! I will tell you where it is, and you may attend my father at the ninth hour. Do not expect to see me there—or again!"

She gave him directions, spun on her heel and walked back the way she had come. He smiled as he watched her go, eyes again drifting of their own accord to below her waist. Perhaps the increased sway of her hips was merely her walking faster to escape his presence the sooner.

CHAPTER 7: THE SINS OF THE FLESH

At the appointed hour Yehuda made his way to Abichail's house. After a deal of good-natured haggling—Abichail did not wish to lose his pots, and Yehuda wanted a reason to return—the deal was set and Yehuda left, whistling as he strolled cheerfully along the street.

Miriam had a subdued dinner with her father. He was not subdued, alternating between discussing where his new pots—acquired at an excellent price, far better than most men could have achieved— would best be displayed, and irritation at the limited mobility imposed by his twisted ankle. Miriam served him, nodded, and spoke little.

Abichail did not wonder at this, for he did not notice it at all.

As it became dark, Miriam retired to her room. She sat at her window, looking out at the darkening city with a yearning for something she dare not name. Finally she extinguished her lamp and lay down to sleep, but it was not a restful one.

Unknown to her, after his meal Yehuda had come back, settling himself into a vantage point in a nearby laneway. He had seen her silhouette in the window as she gazed out into the dusk. Then he smiled, and went home.

~~~

The next week, Miriam's father went to the room where she was pounding grain, a look of grim but optimistic anticipation on his face.

"Daughter. A man has come to me. He says he has looked upon you with favor, and wishes you to be his bride. He has gained my favor. He waits in the courtyard. Come."

Miriam's heart skipped a beat. *Did he dare ask my father? Surely he would not dare. Surely my father would turn a mere potter away?*

"I will come."

She arose and followed him into the courtyard, but her heart sank. It was not Yehuda but another man, somewhat older, named Yonatan. *What demon torments me, with dreams of one man I cannot have, while showering me with others I do not want?* Then a reckless feeling came over her. *Yet this man is not ill-favored. Damn you, Yehuda. You torment my dreams but do not have the courage to seek my hand! You tempt me but offer me no release! I shall accept this man. Then you will leave me alone, and I can forget you.*

So she smiled at the man and listened to his words. When he finished she looked up at her father. "Yes, father. I am content. I shall accept this man as my husband."

A broad grin broke out on the man's face. "Excellent! I shall prepare the documents! I must leave town to inspect my holdings, but I shall return soon for the signing. Farewell, Father. Farewell, Bride."

With that he took his leave. Abichail looked fondly at his daughter, glad that his wayward child had at last seen reason. Miriam looked back at him, her expression one he was familiar with in his own wife's face; one which pleased him. He imagined it an expression of dutiful acceptance of the proper order of things; it was the look of defeat. *Whatever madness or demons have taken my mind, my course is now set, be it to salvation or damnation.*

Then the demon of recklessness doubled down. *Or I will change my mind.*

~~~

Another week passed, during which Miriam did not see Yonatan again. The demons had not let her alone; perhaps when the *ketubbah* was signed and the betrothal was final, they would take the hint and move on to torment someone else. Perhaps they would return to Yehuda and plague him as he deserved.

It was dark but she was not asleep. As much as she would tell herself that Yonatan was more handsome than Yehuda, richer than he, and more desirable in every way: his eyes, the eyes that seemed to want to possess her soul and which her soul desired to be possessed by, would return.

She wished her demons would go to torment him, to turn those eyes into the pain of the unattainable. She did not know that they had both suffered the same ailment since they had first met. Whatever in

Yehuda's past or spirit had coalesced into his unstated ideal of femininity, something about Miriam—perhaps her walk, perhaps the way she held her head, perhaps her eyes—had sent its siren song straight to his soul, bypassing any sense he had left that could have named its folly.

Yehuda had never heard of love at first sight, though the Greeks had written of it and even invented a god to shoot its arrows into the hearts of his victims. But you do not have to know of something to suffer from it.

The affliction is notoriously unreliable. For how can you truly love someone before you know them? He could have expected to forget her, in time: she was just a woman walking past on a public street. Even more he could have expected the illusion to die on his first true meeting with her if ever that happened: the reality of the woman shattering the image of her his mind had constructed from hints and mist.

Miriam did not know why the first sight of him had gripped her own soul. He was just a man, eating a fig, looking at her as she walked. Perhaps it was that his look was neither idle curiosity nor lust, though it held both: perhaps it was the first time a man had looked at her as a human being. Not as a possession, or a servant, or a vehicle for his pleasure, or a means to continue his line: not as a means to anything, just a sight to be looked at for its own sake; a precious life in her own right.

But then he had met her: and the spirit she displayed in her words and expressions had exceeded the promise the sight of her had made.

Even that would not have mattered except to cause him a few months of misery; if only she had not seen the same in him.

Miriam was disturbed by a pattering sound, as of gravel hitting the floor. She listened, but the only sound beside the distant wailing of a baby and barking of some dogs was her father's snoring, to which the dual barriers of distance and curtains were no match. Then it came again, and she rose out of bed to look out the window curiously.

Standing below, gazing up at her room, was Yehuda.

"What are you doing there, you fool!?" she whispered. "My father would whip you if he found you here!"

"Then I am glad you are whispering, so as not to wake him."

"Go away!"

"No."

"Why not?"

"I could not stay away."

"You stayed away this long. Could you not just continue?"

"I tried. I could stand it no longer. Let me up."

"Are you mad? I am a respectable widow, soon to be married!"

Yehuda's face went blank. "Married? Are you betrothed?"

"Not yet, but I am promised. When my future husband returns we shall be betrothed, and you will leave me alone!"

"Do you wish me to leave you alone?"

Miriam was about to give him the reply he deserved, but found she could not. Her twin demons of desire and recklessness were now working together, it seemed. "I... no. No I do not. And it has been my ruin. You invade my dreams and now you invade my house! Why can't you leave me alone?"

"Possibly for the same reason that you do not want me to."

"Oh Yehuda! I am to be married!"

"It is not yet done. You are not yet betrothed, merely promised. Change your mind, and I will make my own offer to your father."

"He would never accept!"

"I will change his mind."

"Yehuda, leave me alone. Why do you torment me thus with promises you cannot keep?"

"Because not seeing you is my torment, one I can bear no more."

Miriam was silent. Her father's snoring still punctuated the night. "Wait."

There was a ladder laid on the roof; Miriam fetched it and fed it quietly out the window. "Come up," she ordered huskily.

When Yehuda stood before her, she did not know what to do. He looked at her with an even greater intensity, as if not merely desiring her soul but devouring it. Her legs felt weak. Her father's snoring added a counterpoint to her thumping heart, as desire and danger ran their twin drumbeats through her veins.

"We are both mad! What will my father do, if he discovers you here?"

"Then we must be quiet. But I cannot go, any more than you can send me away. Do you not feel it too?"

He stood looking at her. "Remove your veil."

She had automatically, incongruously, put her veil on as she waited for him to climb the ladder. Now, feeling as if she were in a dream, she removed it. He reached out, held her cheek in his palm, ran his fingers over her lips, and sighed inaudibly. "Oh, Miriam. How I have wanted to touch you. Since the day I first saw you, I have desired you."

She reached out and touched his face in her turn, running her fingers over his damnable eyes, curling the hairs of his beard around them. "And I... and I, you."

He reached out and held her shoulders. She did not deny him. He lifted her tunic off her body and she stood there, naked. He ran his fingers over her body and it was as if his hands were flame and ice, and she trembled at his touch.

"We must be quiet," she whispered. He nodded, removing his own clothes, and laid her back on her bed.

Then his lips and his hands were on her, and hers on him; and she forgot about engagements and betrothals and law. There was just her and him in the night, as had been between man and woman since the first night of creation. When he entered her, she arched her back; then he began to move in the rhythm she knew, and she felt the familiar frisson of pleasure between her legs. But there was something different about it; he was somehow slower and deeper than her husband had ever been, and she found her pleasure mounting to a height she had never felt. *So my sister wasn't lying after all, if this is what her husband did to her.* And then his rhythm accelerated, and she forgot everything except the feel of his body in hers and the acceleration of her own joy. Then as he shuddered with his final silent thrusts and gasps, it was if a dam broke within her too, and she was so startled by the climactic peak that hit her like a wave that she cried out in shock and ecstasy. *And this must be how he feels, too, when his seed leaves his body. And I never knew. Oh God. No wonder men desire this so.*

But as her orgasm passed, reality returned to her with a crash, and she realized what she had done. "Oh quiet, oh quiet," she whispered desperately to the man still slowly moving inside her, grasping his body with her arms and legs. But she could hear nothing. Her father's snoring had stopped. Then she heard his voice raised querulously, and her blood froze. "Miriam? Miriam! Is that you? What is happening?"

Unfortunately for the two lovers, Abichail's own snoring had briefly lightened his sleep, and an unaccustomed faint thumping sound had disturbed him. As the thumping gained in tempo it disturbed him even more and he woke, puzzled. He was half asleep, and would have drifted off again none the wiser; had not Miriam cried out. He sat up, startled.

He thought perhaps his daughter was in pain or danger, and called out to her; but he knew that rhythm and knew that women in its throes might cry out, for the harlots he occasionally visited sometimes did so to prove their clients' manliness. The knowledge of what was happening in his daughter's room fused into white hot rage. He leapt from his bed and ran towards her room.

She looked at Yehuda, terrified. He looked back at her, eyes wide; she thought it was fear, but knew it was more, though she could not identify its nature.

Yehuda could see the pattern of strategies and futures and none of them were good. Abichail would thrust aside Miriam's curtain within seconds and they would be caught. He was a strict man: though technically the betrothal was not final he would probably consider this adultery, and then anything might happen. Miriam would not, could not, run naked through the streets with him; nor could he abduct her; nor could he defend her. He had to run; but that would leave her here, naked, alone to face her father's rage. He looked into Miriam's eyes, stricken. It was a cowardly act, one she would never forgive; one he would never forgive himself. But it was their only chance: one of them had to remain free and able to act.

"Oh, Miriam, forgive me!" he cried softly. "There is no time! Oh, Miriam!" Then he grabbed up his clothes, darted out the window and down the ladder, and ran off into the night.

Miriam stared after him, unable to understand; then stared at the doorway seconds later as her father's enraged form loomed there like a vengeful angel of God. He looked around the room wildly; at her tunic cast carelessly on the floor, at his daughter on her bed, cover drawn up to her chin to cover her shame. He knew the look and smell of sex and he snarled at her. He ran to the window; looked down; saw the ladder; saw a man running up an alleyway, his pale buttocks flashing shamefully in the moonlight as he vanished into the warren of streets.

Slowly he straightened, turned, and pointed an accusing finger at Miriam's wide eyes. "Harlot! Jezebel! You dare go whoring under my roof!? How long have you been shaming me? How many young men of the town have known you, and laugh at me behind my back?!"

"No, father! I have never! This is the first time since my husband died that I have known a man!"

"You are betrothed!" he roared. Then he stopped, and asked more quietly. "Tell me daughter, on your mother's grave: was that man your betrothed? Is it he who came to take you before the proper time? That is… not unknown. It is… unseemly. But he is your husband, and could not complain as he was party to it. It is not adultery. I could forgive it."

But Miriam shook her head. "No, father. I am sorry. But it was not he."

"Then who was the wicked man?! What man has dared defile my daughter, my household and my name?"

Miriam was still in shock; she was stunned that Yehuda had fled; could not absorb the depth of his betrayal. But she remembered his eyes and the heights to which his body had brought hers. She could not fully believe that he had left her to her fate undefended, even though she now knew it. And though he had betrayed her, still she could not bring herself to betray him. She shook her head, dumbly. "I cannot tell you."

"Were you forced?"

"No."

"Then you are an adulteress!"

"No. I was not yet betrothed. I have sinned against God and the man I was promised to, but it is not adultery."

"You fool! Did you hope to slake your lusts by sneaking your sins beneath a technicality, between promise and signing? Idiot! Harlot! His servant delivered his *ketubbah* and gift for you this afternoon! Yonatan sent him ahead, so eager was he to have you! He was to come tomorrow himself, to give them to you! But they are delivered! You are betrothed!"

Miriam looked at him in horror. She had known what she had done was dangerous but not that it might be deadly. Shame; dishonor; being spurned by Yonatan and cast out by her family: not the finality of death. Her father now held her life in her hands. If she could persuade him to be merciful, he would simply speak to Yonatan and the betrothal would be silently annulled. He would not denounce her; he would despise her, but not publicly shame her. Then she could confess Yehuda's identity and her father might well force them to marry: even now, knowing what Yehuda was, that possibility sent a quiver up her spine.

"Father, please."

"Call me not father. You are no daughter of mine."

"Father, please. I did not know. This man—I love him. I thought I loved him. I do not know what came over me. It is like some demon possessed me and twisted my mind. I just… had to have him. I could not help myself. I am ashamed. But forgive me. Please."

"There is no forgiveness for an adulteress, neither in this world nor the next!"

"Please, Abba. I am flesh of your flesh, life of your life. I did not know I was betrothed; did not know it was adultery. I did not know what I was doing. Forgive me. Have mercy on me, Abba. Have mercy on your daughter."

"You are no daughter of mine." He picked up her tunic, hurled it at her head and turned his back. "Cover your shame!"

Miriam dressed. Then her father grabbed her roughly by the arm and dragged her from her room. "Do not think you can escape justice, whore!"

He dragged her down to the ground level and opened a store room, one with a strong door, used to store tools and valuables. He pushed her in roughly and she fell to the floor; he threw a bucket and thin straw mat in after her, then bolted the door.

"Spend your night in penitence, harlot. Think of the shame you have brought me. Pray to the Lord if you think He will listen."

"Father, Abba, please!" she wailed. But he said nothing, merely lay outside her prison, lest the adulterer return to free her.

She cried, but his ears were closed to any pity. She could not sleep. Her fall, from the heights of ecstasy through the shock of betrayal to the depths of disaster had been so sudden and complete that she could not bear it. *Oh Lord God, why have you destroyed me? Why did you give me such joy, only to tear it down? Was Lucifer's fall from light to shadow so far? Truly I am worthless in your eyes, and there will be no deliverance for me.*

But finally she must have slept, for she opened her eyes to sunlight streaming through the cracks in the door; then she had to cover her face with her arm against the brightness when her father flung the door open. He had had his breakfast; he saw no need to waste food on her.

"Get up!"

"Father, please. I know I am a miserable sinner. But it is in your power to save me. Have mercy on your daughter. I know my betrothed will divorce me. But you do not have to denounce me. You do not have to bear the shame of others knowing. You do not need to watch me die."

"Silence! You will not speak! If shame comes to me I have deserved it, for raising so vile a woman, for being so blind to your whoring!"

He dragged her through the town. People stopped and stared, but dared not ask questions when they saw Abichail's fierce countenance. But when a man looked like that, leading a woman looking like she did, it was not hard to guess the meaning.

He brought her to the leaders of the town and cast her into the dirt. "This is my daughter. Last night I caught her in adultery, in the very act. What is your judgment?"

The men inspected her. She looked back, eyes filled with fear, leaking tears. At first they did not speak to her.

"There is no doubt?"

"I heard it. I saw her nakedness. I saw the man running away, having used our ladder to enter then escape. The ladder was kept in my dwelling so she must have provided it for him. She was complicit."

"Who was the adulterer?"

"She will not say."

Now one of them addressed her. "You will not say? The man is a coward who ran away, leaving you to your fate. Denounce him too, as is your duty to your father, your husband and your God."

But Miriam just shook her head.

"Speak, woman!"

"I will not say."

The man spat on the ground. "Has she any defense?"

"She says a demon entered her mind and made her do it."

The man smirked. "Convenient, to blame a demon we cannot see. Perhaps it is true. But if so, she let it in. Her own lusts were the key it used to unlock her spirit and her thighs."

"Perhaps that is why she will not denounce the man," another suggested. "Perhaps the demon stills her tongue, that its other servant may escape."

"Have you anything to say in your defense?"

"I beg for mercy. I did not know I was betrothed. I am ashamed; I sinned, for I knew what I was doing; but I did not know it was adultery!"

"She was betrothed!" her father answered harshly. "If she did not know the betrothal was sealed, yet she had already made her promise, of her own free will. It is the same."

The men nodded.

Miriam saw that Yonatan had arrived, fetched by some servant or other. Guilt twisted in her belly as she saw him; but there was neither pain nor pity in his eyes, just contempt and condemnation. Perhaps that indicated the kind of husband he would have been. Or perhaps any man betrayed in such a manner would be the same.

"So what is your verdict?" asked Abichail.

They looked at each other and at Miriam, who looked back with terror: she saw no mercy in their eyes.

"She has committed adultery. She will be stoned to death."

Miriam sat back with a sigh of despair. Then one of the men interposed, "But there is still her ignorance. It gives some latitude. Her betrothed may choose to ignore the evidence," he said, looking to Yonatan. In truth, the only reason he would was if he were the one who had lain with her. The woman had denied it—but what was the word or reasons of a woman? But Yonatan merely shook his head curtly. "Or," the man said, now addressing Abichail, "as her father, you have the right to plead for mercy; give her a lesser punishment than death."

"Stand, woman. That I may look upon you," commanded Abichail.

Miriam stood, quivering. Abichail looked her up and down, lips curled in contempt, remembering what he had seen last night.

"Father! Abba!" she cried softly, pleadingly.

For a moment she saw his eyes soften, as a memory returned to him of a little girl perched on his knee, eyes looking adoringly into his. But then he remembered the creature she had become, and any pity he felt for her fear, any feeling he had for the flesh of his flesh, merely inflamed his righteous hatred at what she now was. His eyes became as agate and he reached out and pushed her to the ground, ripping the front of her tunic as he did so. "I fear God. I grant no mercy to adulterers. Let all the world now see your shame, woman! If you seek mercy, seek it from the God whose laws you have despised."

The chief man of the group again stood forward. "It is decided. But she will have time to reflect on her sin. Lock her up. Give her water that she may not die, but no food. Perhaps she will denounce the adulterer. In any case, she dies in the hour before sunset."

~~~

When the sun was sinking in the sky the men dragged her through the street to the place of stoning, a small crowd collecting in their wake. They threw her to the ground and the men stood around her in a rough circle. She sat in the dirt supporting her weight on one arm while trying

46

to hold her ripped tunic over her breasts with the other. Her eyes pleaded for mercy but she said nothing; she knew neither the pleas of her eyes nor any pleas of her mouth would be answered.

She swallowed, mouth dry. *So now my life ends, without seeing my twentieth year. I have worshipped the Lord to the best of my lights all my life. What possessed me to throw it all away on a worthless man, who wanted only to spend his own passion in my body then leave me to my fate? Curse you Yehuda of Kerioth, curse you to the end of time, for your eyes and your passion, your lies and betrayals! Yet... Yet you drew out from me a passion and joy I never knew could be possessed or felt by mortal woman. Perhaps then in some small way you redeemed my life, even as you ended it.*

Unknown to her, Yehuda was watching from the shadows, his eyes and mind calculating. He was armed with his *sicara;* if any of the men surrounding Miriam could match his weapon, he doubted they could match his skill honed by years with the caravan. But then what?

That "then what?" had been his constant companion all day, first when she was dragged to her trial, then when she was held prisoner, and now. If he could have gone up to them with his weapon and rescued Miriam from their murderous clutches, what could he achieve with the crowd in hot pursuit?

She had never been left unguarded so he had never had the chance to steal her away. There had been one occasion when he felt hope. There must have been a commotion in another part of the town, for on hearing some news most of the men had run off in great excitement. But two had remained in the compound, less interested or more dutiful than the rest. Between surprise and his *sicara,* he probably could have slain those two and been away before his crime was detected. But two adulterers had little enough chance of escape; two murderers had even less, and Miriam herself was unlikely to accept such a horrific rescue.

If he could have stolen a horse perhaps they might have fled into the wilderness with their lives; but horses were few and well guarded, and he had found none he could steal. A lesser animal like a donkey would be worthless. No, they would have to escape by foot, and how could two people on foot escape a crowd swarming after them in holy rage? If they were fast, and very lucky, perhaps they could find a hiding place in the rocky wilderness beyond. But they would never get there alive.

And if they did? How could two people survive in that wilderness, with the town and soon the surrounding area in uproar? With every man's sword turned against them? Join a band of robbers? He would probably end up dead, and she raped or dead or both. Neither the law nor the lawless could help them now.

So all day he had watched and waited, hoping for a chance to present itself that would do more than quicken both their deaths. He had found no answer. His talent at seeing the patterns swirling around in the chaos mocked him, seeing nothing but the certainty of the tomb.

And so shall I leave her to die, believing she is abandoned by all men; to die alone in shame and terror? When I have betrayed her, yet still she has not betrayed me?

Perhaps he would simply march up to them. Shout to them. Confess his own sin. He could declare his love for her; say how he went to her that night to plead his own case before her; how she had agreed, not knowing her betrothal had been set; how in their joy they had lost control of their minds. Perhaps then they would forgive. But looking at them, at their rage and hunger, he knew they would not. Instead of one stoning there would be two, for he was as guilty of adultery as she.

So is the price of my life to abandon her, terrified and alone and betrayed? What then is my own life worth? No. I will face the crowd. I will plead our case. Perhaps the Lord Most High will hear my words, and will soften the hearts of the crowd. But if not, my love will know she was not betrayed; is not alone; is not abandoned. It is better to die as a man than live as a cur.

He drew out his *sicara*, knowing it would at least win him a hearing. But then he heard a rising hubbub from the crowd and a shouting from the street beyond. The men around Miriam turned to look. So Yehuda sheathed his sword and waited to see the form of this temporary reprieve.

Chapter 8: Without Sin

From the shouts of the crowd, Yehuda realized that some kind of prophet had entered the town, and this must have been the commotion that granted him false hope earlier. These itinerant holy men were not uncommon; the more oppressed the people felt, the more prophets arose to either berate them for their sins or comfort them with promises of deliverance.

Yehuda had little patience for them. He had met a number in his wide travels. He worshipped his God as he had been raised to do, but he would not have said that religion clung to him tightly. He was too cynical about the nature of men and priests, and the more they put on airs of superiority, like the Pharisees, the more he saw hypocrisy. He had seen few exceptions to this rule. Men were men, with the foibles and weaknesses common to the race. Some tried harder than others, but those who were the most genuine were, in Yehuda's experience, the least likely to look down their smug noses at others.

His cynicism about holy men was equally born of experience. Many of his more gullible fellows seemed to think that the more intense the conviction or the wilder the eyes, the closer to God a prophet was. In Yehuda's view, yet to be contradicted by reality, it meant closer to madness instead. They all attracted their fanatical adherents who could not see why the rest of the world refused to follow them. And then they all faded away. They fell, to exposure or snakebite. They became truly mad, and wandered away forever. The crowd turned on them when their miracles or prophecies failed. Or if none of that claimed them, sometimes those in power would begin to fear them and find some pretext on which to end their careers.

Then Yehuda remembered the strange man who had stood on a cliff face watching him as he went to collect clay for Lucius, some months ago now. His contempt for holy men failed to touch that memory. He could not say why, but something in his isolation and the intensity of his shrouded gaze still made Yehuda shiver, as if in the presence of something ineffable.

Who that man was, perhaps Yehuda would never know. The most famous one he had heard of was one Yohanan, the Baptizer. His hook was baptism: the ritual cleansing of sin by immersion in water. His popularity bore witness to the true nature of men: if they could find something as simple to wash away their sins as being dunked in a river, then that was far preferable to doing anything about the sinning. In fairness to Yohanan he preached that the baptism was not the end of virtue but the start of a new, redeemed life; but Yehuda wondered how many of those he baptized even got as far as their own homes before they returned to their accustomed ways.

At the thought, Yehuda again looked with contempt at the crowd still surrounding Miriam, wondering what multitude of secret sins those men hid, these men who would righteously crush Miriam's life from her for one sin of hers.

Whoever the fellow slowly getting closer was, he wasn't Yohanan: that one did not need to seek people out, they sought him out at his river, the holy Jordan. Yehuda wondered what this one's hook was. He could not see him: the preacher was of average height, well screened by onlookers. From what he could see in following the man's progress among the shifting crowd, the preacher must be at the height of his popularity: he had a retainer of men, several wearing the road-worn look of those who had traveled long distances through the countryside.

The crowd were excited and the men around Miriam waited with anticipation, their hands stayed for now. The one thing more popular than a stoning was a stoning attended by a holy man, who could harangue the condemned and with luck the crowd as well. The crowd loved to be told of their sins: it made them feel holier by the act of deigning to listen.

Finally the prophet reached the circle of men and he stopped. He looked around the crowd. It seemed to Yehuda that his eyes stopped on him, though surely the man could not see him. Yet he stared in his direction for long seconds, before continuing his examination of the crowd. Or perhaps it was Yehuda's own reality that paused.

For at the sight he had gasped. There was something in the black intensity of that gaze which rocked him to his core. He had seen it before. But what crazy holy man could it have been?

Then his mind removed the beard, reshaped the man's face to the rounder one of a boy. A boy he had known.

"Yeshua!" he breathed. "My God! It is Yeshua!"

Yeshua finished his examination of the crowd, who were now silent, or as silent as crowds can be, eagerly awaiting his next move. If he proved to be a false prophet, there might even be another stoning, for blasphemy!

When Yehuda had known him his voice was that of a boy. His laughter that of a boy. Now his voice rang out, clear and commanding. Whether it was the natural result of puberty or he had trained it, Yehuda did not know. Nor did he care. The voice held him just as the eyes had. Just as it now held the people of the town in its strange thrall.

"What are you doing here, people of Magdala?"

Yonatan stepped forward. Any love he may have thought he felt for Miriam was dust, and he was an educated man; he looked forward to a verbal duel with a prophet. At worst, he would be taught; at best, he would win and gain much status in the town for his wisdom.

"This woman was found in adultery. She is to be stoned, as says the law."

"Will nobody speak for her?" he said, again staring in Yehuda's direction like an accusation. But he could not move, as if pinned by Yeshua's eyes.

"She has no defense. She was caught in the act, and has confessed it. She claims to be deceived by demons, but if the demons have taken her, let them have her."

"Let me see her."

Miriam looked up at him as the circle parted to let him through and he approached. If normal men would not grant her mercy, she knew a holy man certainly would not. If anything he would excoriate her for every sin she had committed since leaving her mother's breast. He would probably throw the first stone himself, beginning the dreadful hail which would end her life.

But when she looked into his eyes, she fell into their black pools. If Yehuda looked at her as if to possess her soul, this man looked at her as if he owned it already and could see it, weigh it, judge it and refine it. And if the slightest virtue then remained, never throw it away. Never vanish into the darkness taking her virtue and her life with him as he ran.

"What is your name, woman?"

"I am Miriam, widow of Binyamin, daughter of…" she looked at her father's face, stony in its refusal. "Daughter of none. I have sinned, but I knew it not. Have mercy on me, Holy One."

"They say you are possessed by demons. Is this true? Is that your excuse for breaking the laws of God and Man?"

She could not lie to those eyes; she could only say the truth. "I do not know. All I know is that something possessed me but I know not what. It was more than lust, though lust I am guilty of. It was a passion too deep for me to fathom; love for an unworthy man, who used me then betrayed me. I promised myself in marriage to another man, to escape him. But still he sought me out, and still I lay with him. But I did not know I was yet betrothed, Master! I did not know! I did not know I committed adultery!"

His eyes bored into her. "And if you had known? If this man had come to you? Would you have called out? Would you have denounced him? Or would you have lain with him still?"

Miriam gasped. This man was pulling her soul apart thread by thread; lies she did not know herself he now exposed to the world. "I… I would have. Nothing could have saved me from my doom."

"Rise, woman!" he commanded. "Hear your judgment!"

Miriam rose, uncertain of what would come next but powerless to disobey.

He turned to address the crowd. "Behold the woman! You have heard her words! Has any man here had previous cause to question this woman's virtue? She is a widow. Did not her marriage bed produce the proofs of virginity, as is required by law?"

The crowd muttered, but none could raise an accusation or deny his words.

"Then who among you would deny demons have corrupted her?"

Nobody answered, enthralled by his reasoning.

"Who among you could resist the power of a demon, if it chose to torment you?" he asked in ringing challenge.

Again he looked around the crowd. Each one on whom his eyes rested averted theirs, in shame and submission.

Then he said softly, so the crowd had to strain to hear, "The Son of Man can resist demons. By the power of the Holy Spirit, the Son of Man can cast them out!"

With that he put his hand on Miriam's forehead. As he cried out "Depart this woman, who is God's servant!" his hand moved quickly. Though its motion seemed too little to have any effect, Miriam fell to the ground with a loud cry.

Yeshua again looked around the crowd. "No demons torment her now. What then should become of her?"

Yonatan again spoke up; but uncertainly, looking around to judge the support of the crowd. "So you say, prophet. But who can say the demons will not return when you go? Or that they did not enter her because she was ready for them, her heart already full of lust and betrayal? Demons or no, she is guilty of adultery by her own words. Would you not uphold the law?"

"Surely justice must be done! So let there be justice. Let he who is without sin among you throw the first stone."

Yeshua again raked the crowd with his gaze, and again they would not meet his eyes. They all felt something in the air; a chill, as of a judgment higher than their own; a judgment they could not face; a judgment that would return on their own heads whatever decision they rendered today. First one, then another, hung his head and left.

Finally only two were left of those who had gathered to cast stones, her betrothed and her father. Yonatan looked around nervously. He saw no support in the remaining onlookers, only a watchful curiosity about whether he would throw a stone, whether that meant he claimed to be without sin, and what they might do if he did. The prophet's men had looks more pointed; two of them especially, brothers by the look of them, glared at him sternly with muscled arms crossed and eyes threatening. Finally Yonatan spat on the ground in Miriam's general direction and departed. Abichail spared one last look of loathing for his daughter, spun on his heels and followed him.

His disciples and some of the crowd still looked on, wondering. Yeshua bent to pick up a stone and threw it; Miriam flinched but it bounced past her harmlessly. The onlookers looked at each other, wondering what this meant. Did this man claim to be without sin? Or was he merely expressing his contempt for the woman—or the men who would have stoned her?

Then he looked down on her and said, simply, "Go and sin no more."

With one last look around, he gestured to his men to follow him and walked away without a further glance.

Miriam still looked up at him as he went, wide eyed. "Wait! Wait! Where shall I go?"

Yeshua turned to look at her. "Wherever you will."

"All faces are turned against me. I would follow you, Master. Wherever you go, I shall follow you."

"I will not be your Master," he replied sternly, turning and striding away. Miriam bowed her head, in sorrow or shame. Then after a few more steps, he added without turning around, "That does not mean you may not follow me."

She ran after him and prostrated herself, holding his feet and kissing them.

"You have saved me. I shall follow you to the ends of the Earth."

He reached down his hand and lifted her up. "Then rise, Miriam of Magdala. Come. Leave all your goods behind you and follow me."

"Wait, my lord. From my husband I received a generous *ketubbah;* while I live it is mine to do with as I will. It will be my gift to you, to help you in your ministry. Wealth is no use to the dead, and dead I should now be. All I have is yours."

A large man, with clear eyes and the air of a leader of men, stepped forward from among the disciples. "We do not seek wealth, woman. The Lord God provides all our needs."

Yeshua reached out and touched the man gently on the shoulder. "Peace, Shimon. If we wish the Lord to provide, should we close our eyes when he has done so? Let the woman make her gift." He turned to the two who had cast their stern eyes on Yonatan. "Yaakov, Yohanan! Accompany her to her father's house and fetch her property. Ensure she is not molested. Then meet us at the camp."

The men nodded and departed with Miriam as guide, while Yeshua turned and strode off with his men toward the setting sun.

As they headed down an alleyway a man stepped out in front of them to bar their way. Visible at his waist was a *sicara,* one of unusual size and quality. Some of the disciples reached toward their own weapons, but Yeshua held up his hand to them and waited.

"Yeshua of Nazareth," the man said, a statement not a question.

"Yehuda of Kerioth."

"Yes."

"It has been many years, my friend. Are you still as impudent?"

"It has been many years, my friend. Are you still as arrogant?"

The men smiled, and clasped hands. "Come Yehuda, sup with us. We were boys and now we are men. Let us learn what we have done with those years, and what they have done to us."

Yehuda lifted Yeshua's hand to his lips and kissed it. "I told you I would kiss your hand on the day I came to follow you. I will follow you, Yeshua. For what you have done today, I will follow you to hell and back."

Yeshua gestured to his men to go on ahead. When the two were alone he spoke again.

"It was you, was it not?"

Yehuda stared at him. It seemed to be Yeshua's style, to leave things unsaid and let the listener fill in the meaning themselves, from their own passions or their own guilt. But this was terse even for him. Yehuda wondered if that was a mark of respect for his mind—or contempt for his guilt. But he had been coward enough for one day, and would not ask the meaning.

"No betrayal was intended, as no adultery was intended; but betray her I did, and for it I may never be forgiven."

"If you betrayed her, perhaps you will betray me also. Perhaps I should refuse your offer. You are a dangerous man, Yehuda, and not only for the blade you carry."

"I would never betray you, Yeshua."

"And yesterday: would you not have said the same to her?"

CHAPTER 9: THE KINGDOM OF HEAVEN

When Miriam arrived at the camp with Yaakov and Yohanan carrying her worldly goods behind her, she was mortified to see Yehuda also there. *He fears that I denounced him; he sees that my lord Yeshua is a man of mercy; so he runs like the coward he is. Must he dog me to the end of my days?*

He was staring at her with his usual intensity, as if at a sight he had thought never to see again, though surely he knew that she had joined Yeshua's band. She looked away, refusing his gaze. *Do not look at me, Yehuda of Kerioth. We are done. Then why do my soul and body still yearn for him? Do the demons still gather around me, waiting for their chance to defile me again? I shall not look upon his face. And Yeshua will protect me. While I am in his presence, neither demon nor Yehuda can harm me.*

Yehuda watched her turn away, his heart yearning to tell her the truth: to tell her he had not abandoned her. But she would not believe him. He did not truly believe it himself.

~ ~ ~

When Miriam had asked to follow Yeshua, all she had felt was the relief of her redemption, and all she had thought of were the hypnotic eyes of the man who had saved her. It had not even occurred to her to think of the propriety of an unmarried woman travelling with a group of virile young men. Perhaps it was strange that such considerations would matter to her at all given the circumstances of her rescue. But she was at heart how she had described herself to Yehuda, a respectable, moral woman, despite her one fall into lust and ecstasy.

So as she walked, first to her former home and then to Yeshua's camp, she began to worry about what might befall her there: a lone, young and helpless woman among men, whose lusts she now knew so well.

So she was relieved, if surprised, to discover other women had preceded her. Women were considered barely above animals; it was rare for a holy man to notice them, let alone accept them amongst his disciples. *Who is this Yeshua,* she wondered? *What manner of man is he?*

The women shared their own tent and Miriam was welcomed among them. They explained their life to her. Women might be welcome, but their roles were much the same as elsewhere. They tended to the men, prepared food, mended clothes. But that might have been simply because it is what they were trained to do, for they also learned: Yeshua spoke to all people, male or female, as worthy disciples. It was as if he did not notice their sex; as if the differences in their bodies did not matter when he spoke to their souls.

One thing truly startled her. She was relieved to learn that the women were not expected to engage in sexual relations with the men; that niggling possibility for why Yeshua was so tolerant of female followers could be put to rest. But as he had forgiven her so had Yeshua forgiven others the world deemed sinners, and one of his followers had been a prostitute. Prostitutes were accepted in society: a man could have sex with whomever he pleased, as long as she was a woman and not another man's wife. If he was married his wife might punish him for it in her own way, but the worst he would get from his neighbors would be contempt from the more upright ones, not a stoning. It was a sin but not a fatal one.

In one of the towns Yeshua had passed through a prostitute named Shelomit had heard him talk; had her heart touched by his message of redemption. She had given up her sinful ways and followed him.

Yeshua had forbidden his men from using prostitutes. But his reasons had not been grounded in the virtues of chastity. Rather, he knew his message would ruffle feathers, especially among the religious authorities. "I am already bringing a sword," he told his followers. "If we are to be attacked, let us be attacked for what is important, not for distractions. The Priests and Pharisees will discredit us any way they can. Let them try by attacking our message, where we are strong. Let us not give them weapons out of our own hands, forged by our own weakness."

Men were men, and some could bear chastity better than others.

One night one of the disciples had secretly approached Shelomit.

"Lay with me," he said.

"I have left that life behind me."

"You have known many men. Will one more matter?"

"I have not known a man in that way since I joined you."

"I need it. I will not insult you by offering money and I cannot demand it of you. But I ask it of you."

She softened. It had been a long time since she had lain with a man, and this man was not repulsive. She sighed. "Very well, lay with me. But Yeshua must not know. He might forgive us, but I do not wish to have to ask. Even less do I wish him to feel I have betrayed his mercy or his trust."

And so they had lain together. But Yeshua somehow knew, as he seemed to know so many things. As they lay entwined on the ground afterwards he had appeared out of the moonlight. Shelomit had gasped, wondering what words of condemnation he might offer; whether perhaps he would cast them out of his camp and his life. But he had looked down at them, nodded, and said simply, "It is well," before returning the way he had come.

Yeshua said nothing of it, but some secrets cannot hide. One night in the wilderness, as he sat away from the others on a hillock thinking his thoughts, his disciples came to him.

"Lord, we have heard what you did when you found Shelomit lying with one of us. We do not understand."

Yeshua beckoned them to sit. "What did I do?"

The man who had taken Shelomit said, "Nothing. You did nothing."

"No. I said it was well. Hear me! The Kingdom of God is not of this world, and when it comes women will not be given in marriage nor shall men take them in marriage. Is it not written that the trials and tribulations of men, the rites of marriage and the pain of childbirth, followed the expulsion of Adam and Eve from the Garden? Yet is it not written that before their fall they were as one flesh?"

The disciples made no answer.

"For a man to lie with a woman was God's plan from the beginning of time. Do you not know it in your own flesh? Do you imagine the Lord Most High granted you such glory to torment you?

"Do you still not understand? There are reasons why men marry and why adultery and fornication are sins. But those reasons lie in the world of men; the world ushered in by the Fall. While you are with me, you live in the Kingdom of Heaven on Earth. It is a taste of things to come. There are crimes against God. There are crimes against men. None of these may be permitted in the Kingdom of Heaven, because they are crimes: as Lucifer learnt when his pride misled him. But for a man to lie with a woman with her consent is not one of them. It is a crime in the Kingdom of Man, for a man must be sure his sons are his. But it is to the pleasure of God in the Kingdom of Heaven, for it is his gift to us, intended for our pleasure. Our joy is His joy, for we are His children."

The men and women hearing these words gaped, for they had never heard the like from any other rabbi.

"So I tell you this. If any woman here wishes to lie with one of you: she may, and it is a sin for neither. If any man wishes to lie with one of you women, and you find him pleasing: he may, and it is a sin for neither. In doing this you celebrate God and his glory: therefore your act is holy.

"But men! Most of you have wives. You must honor them, as is their due. When we are near your own place, lie only with your wife. Do not dishonor her by lying with another when you may seek her out for your pleasure and hers."

They sat there, staring at him; wondering at his words.

"You are my inner circle and these words are only for you. Others would not understand; others are not to know. Not ever. The Kingdom of Heaven is not yet; except only while you are with me. Now go, and consider my words."

Slowly they arose; walked off in twos and threes, looking back at him but none choosing to speak. He stayed, continuing his meditations.

Yeshua knew the power of sex. Its use in religion from temple prostitutes to the practices of cults, from bizarre Dionysian orgies to strict celibacy, attested to it. This secret rite would tie his people together even more than his words and their faith. He did not fear sexual jealousy. When men were free to choose, how could it arise?

~~~

Miriam heard this tale, mouth hanging open.

The tale done, the women looked at her, smiling; waiting for the questions they knew would come.

"Have you... have you all done this?" she finally asked when her head stopped spinning.

"No. More than one, less than all."

"And the men? All of them?"

"Most. Not all."

"How often is it demanded of you?"

"It is never demanded, only asked. Often enough, but not too often. They are restrained. They are not like husbands, who come home every night or two demanding their due. To them it is holy; precious in its rarity. It is strange. It is as if, having been granted the right, it means more to them the less they indulge. But do not mistake me, Miriam. It is the same for us."

"Are they ever refused?"

"Sometimes. But they are not angry; they ask elsewhere."

"And if none of you will lie with them?"

"Then they accept it, and ask again another night."

"What about Yeshua? Have you lain with him?"

The women all shook their heads. "I asked him," said one. "He has never asked it of us, but I asked him. He would not."

"Did he give a reason?"

"He said he awaited the one God had chosen for him."

CHAPTER 10: CHOICES

Weeks passed. Yeshua's ministry was growing, his fame spreading. The people of the towns and villages along the way began to await his arrival with great anticipation. A trickle began to flow toward him even from more distant towns. Yehuda wondered what would happen when the trickle became a flood.

Miriam continued to avoid him. When she could not she did what she had to do, but she would not look at him. She would not speak to him. He did not try to force her. If her love for him had gone, he would bear the torture of his love for her as his just punishment. In the face of her indifference it would wither soon enough. But it showed no sign of dying yet.

Miriam still felt the presence of the demons that taunted her with memories of Yehuda. It could be bad during the day, if she should see him and her defenses of contempt and indifference were down. It could be worse during the night, if the demons brought her dreams of him; especially if in those dreams he lay with her and nobody came to tear them apart for their sin. Sometimes she would awake from such a dream desperate for his presence, knowing he slept mere yards away from her; knowing she could go to him. Knowing that if she did, he would reach for her, draw her down to him, and bring her to that peak of delight which she had known but once, but could never forget.

She would be damned if she did.

But when she was with Yeshua there were no demons. There was only Yeshua with his kind wisdom and eyes in which she could drown but never die. He did not seek much; he did not demand that others tend to him more than to his fellows; he did not demand that others wash his feet. But nor would he refuse it if it was offered: he knew that they did it to honor him, and that he honored them by accepting.

One night she brought with her a bowl, and began to wash his feet. She did not know what this feeling was that held her; she just knew that the tender way she washed away the dirt and tension was enough for her, possibly enough for her always.

Then she looked up at his face to smile at him, and her breath caught in her throat. She knew the look in his eyes, a look she had never hoped to see in them; knew it reflected the look in her own.

She bowed her head, face reddening, mind confused. But he put his finger under her chin and lifted up her face, then said just one gentle word: "Yes."

It was concise even for him, but she knew what it meant. Knew that he meant not only its literal meaning, but more: an affirmation of her, of her worthiness, of her virtue. But all those were themselves condensed back into the literal meaning, and its immediacy was almost too much to bear.

Trembling, she stood up, and took his hand. He stood too, and led her into the wilderness.

They walked through the night, the light of a quarter moon casting its silver sheen over the land. They said nothing. Nothing needed to be said; his one word still hung between them like a blessing or a promise.

They found a comfortable, private spot; an area of sandy soil covered by a layer of soft herbaceous plants in the shelter of a small tree. There they sat, and Miriam, experienced with only two men in her life and each so different, wondered what the third would bring.

Yehuda was skilled in the arts of love. Much of it he had learned from harlots. They were expert in how to please a man, and glad to teach a man how to please a woman; and Yehuda had been a keen student. Even harlots appreciated a man giving them pleasure, and he knew that a woman's enjoyment was likely to rebound upon himself.

Miriam did not know that; nor did she know what training or native skill Yeshua might possess. All she knew, as she welcomed him into her soul and her body, was that she was lucky a second time, as he elicited from her flesh the pleasure she had felt with Yehuda, and the indescribable pinnacle it could reach. As it approached she knew what it was, knew what to expect; this time she did not cry out, or not so loudly. But it did not matter. This time there was no one to hide from;

there were none to find her, none to condemn her, none to damn her. It was just she and he, bodies entwined under the tree, the moon and the stars, as they lay bathed in the fading glory of their union.

After a while he stood, lifted her up and they dressed. Then they walked back to the camp. Still not a word had passed between them. That single "yes" was enough for them both.

~~~

Yehuda had been sitting on a rock, looking out over a valley, occasionally throwing a rock just to hear it bounce down the slope and kick up its own retinue of smaller stones. *The parable of the stones,* he thought wryly.

He had been thinking of Miriam. Wishing she would leave him alone, even though that was precisely what she had been doing. Wishing he could forget her. Forget her eyes, the smoothness of her skin, the softness of her breasts… *Stop it! That is not the way to forget, but to regret. Give it up, Yehuda. She is gone forever.*

He had seen Yeshua and Miriam walk out into the wilderness beyond the camp together. He knew what it meant, what they would do there: and it had been like a knife in his belly, releasing a flood. The flood he identified as hate. *Why do I hate them?* he thought. *I could have had her. All I had to do was go to her father, seeking betrothal. If he had spurned me, and if she had loved me enough, we did not need his permission. She is a widow, of age; perhaps not a thing done, but a thing able to be done. Instead I came to her as a thief in the night, stole her virtue from her, caused her to lose all: her father, her reputation, her life. It haunts me, the thought of Yeshua with her, flesh on flesh. But without Yeshua her flesh would now be cold and dead, food for the worm. He delivered her where I could not; he saved her when I condemned her; he has earned her love. Perhaps it is not them but myself I hate.*

He had sat there, throwing his rocks and thinking his dark thoughts, he knew not how long. Then he saw them come back together, and he knew the knife had not lied and his thoughts were true. He snarled in rage at the sky. *Lord of Hosts, will you never tire of tormenting me? He is the man I love most in the world; she the woman I love most. Must I lose the one to the other? Must I lose both?*

He did not think Yeshua could have seen him. The pair were too wrapped in each other's presence, the moonlight too dim, his vantage too dark and distant. But a short while after Yeshua and Miriam had been lost to view he heard the faint scuff of sandals coming nearer, and turned to see Yeshua approaching. *Damn you. Is there nothing you do not see? I do not need your knife joining hers. Leave me alone!*

But he said none of that, merely gestured for Yeshua to sit, dreading his words.

"You love her."

Yehuda made no reply. What was the point?

"She hates you."

"I know it."

"She hates you because she loves you."

"You excel yourself tonight with your riddles," he snapped.

Yeshua was silent.

"I am sorry," Yehuda said.

"It is no matter. I understand your anger. But she hates you because she loves you; she cannot bear the love, so she tries to bury it in hate."

Yehuda was silent. After a while Yeshua spoke again.

"Tell me. Tell me all."

Yehuda sighed. "To what end? It is past; dead as our love."

"Tell me."

"Very well. I knew if I stayed with her to face her father we were both doomed. I thought if I escaped I would be free to save her if she were indeed condemned. I did not think she would be, but I feared her father's strictness and wrath. I did not run out of fear; I ran to give us both a chance if my fears proved true."

"Yet you did not come back for her. When I arrived she was about to die."

"I could find no plan to save her. I was about to go to her, to confess my part in it, to plead with those holy bastards for her life."

"Then you would both be dead."

"Probably. But I could not leave her to die, alone and betrayed. I would save her or if not, at least spare her that. At least I would die a man."

Yeshua was silent a while before he replied.

"I have many disciples, Yehuda of Kerioth. But of them all, I love you the most. It has always been thus, from our first meeting in the streets of Jerusalem. Have you not felt it—old friend?

"But of all women, I love Miriam of Magdala the most. I wish it were not so, that I could return her to you. But I love her, and cannot let her go, any more than you could if given the choice."

"It is set then. I could not ask it even if you were willing. She has made her own choice."

Again there was a long pause before Yeshua answered.

"Do not despair, my friend. The Lord's ways are mysterious. Do not think that I have taken Miriam from you. Think of her life as a journey. She has taken a different path for now, but perhaps that path will lead her back to you."

"How is that possible? You love her, you say. You are a greater man than I. All men are heroes of their own tale, is that not true? Yet even I cannot stand before you and not recognize who is the greater man. I could no more ask you or her to change your love than I can change mine. I could no more take her from you than I could nail you to a tree."

"Have you heard the legend of Akhilleus?"

"No."

"It is a Greek legend. I heard it from a Greek teacher some years ago now. It is said that his gods gave him a choice: he could choose glory but die young, or choose a long and peaceful life and be forgotten. He chose the former: hence his name is still sung of, though he has been dead for centuries."

"What is the point of your tale?"

"Men such as I are not fated to live long, Yehuda. I stir the hornet's nest. I speak truth to those who do not want it. I will be loved. But I will also be hated. I will be denied, I will be betrayed, and even those who call my name will call for my death."

"Then why do you do it? Is what you think you can achieve worth your own death?"

"Why were you willing to face down a crowd for Miriam, even if you could not save her, even if all you could do was give her a happier death—not alone, but knowing she was loved to the end?"

"You know why."

"Then you know my reasons too. We all must choose our path, Yehuda. I must do what I have come into the world to do. The other disciples do not see it yet. They are filled with the Spirit of God, glorying in the strides we are making. They do not see that it must end. They do not need to see it yet."

"But if it will end, what is your purpose? If you know you will fail, why do you still strive?! Save yourself, Yeshua! Take Miriam, take her with my blessing, take her back to your home. Live your life! Have your children! Even if I am never to see either of you again—go!"

"It will end, but it will not fail. I will die, but something greater will arise from the ashes."

"How can you know that?! How can you know any of it?!"

But Yeshua would not answer. Finally he spoke.

"We are of one soul, you and I, Yehuda of Kerioth. You would die to defend the woman you love, yet you would send me away with her even if it meant you would never see her again. I knew it. I knew that spirit was within you. That is why I love you, and you me."

For a while Yehuda sat there in silence, again casting stones into the night. One hit with a loud crack, shattering into fragments. Perhaps it had some inherent flaw, ready to fail at the first test. Or perhaps it had struck a harder stone, one so adamantine that any lesser one must crumble at its touch. *The parable of the stones, indeed.* "But what will remain of me," he asked quietly, "after I have sacrificed all that I love?"

"Sacrifice?" asked Yeshua even more quietly; so softly Yehuda could barely hear him. "Is it sacrifice?"

His eyes bored into Yehuda's with that look which measured souls. Then he spoke again, still low but with a strange intensity.

"Were you going to face down the crowd because you wanted to die? Or was it to save the life of the woman you loved, whatever the risk to you? Knowing that if you failed, at least you would die as a man? And more: knowing there is no other way for a man to live?"

Yehuda glanced at him, startled.

"Yes, my friend. I do not tell men to give up their wealth to gain the Kingdom of Heaven because I want them to be poor. I tell it to those who value their gold more than their soul, to shine the light on the choice they face. The Kingdom of Heaven is worth more than all else. I do not tell men to be like a man who throws his gold into the sea, but to be like the man who would sell all he owns to buy a pearl beyond price.

"But when I say these things, men have no ears to hear. They think I speak of sacrifice because they do not see past the cost to the gain. If sacrifice is virtue then I would give Miriam up for your happiness. But love you as I do, I will not: for I love her even more. I cannot give her up."

"Yet you are willing to give up your life!"

"Do you think the choice Akhilleus made, the choice I must make, is sacrifice? Any man who loves his life will choose its purpose, Yehuda: the purpose to which his life is dedicated, that which he wishes to achieve above all else. If the price of that purpose becomes my life itself, then so be it. Not because I want to die, but to give birth to a greatness that will transcend my life.

"Understand this, my friend. There is no sacrifice: there is only price."

They were silent for a while. Then Yeshua spoke again.

"Yehuda, you have not sacrificed Miriam or your love for her. If I had stolen Miriam from you by lies and tricks you would not let me take her. You would fight for her with all the power at your command. But you do not fight, because you know Miriam has made her choice. You do not fight for her because she is no longer yours. That is your greatness, Yehuda. Not that you are willing to give her up, but why: though you had never learned the words to name it.

"So do not despair, Yehuda. I love Miriam, and I will have her, but I know I cannot keep her for long. One day I will be gone; and if on that day she knows betrayal is not in your nature, on that day she will return to you."

CHAPTER 11: DISCIPLES

It was not long before Miriam's intimate relationship with Yeshua was known throughout the band. It was not a secret, nor a matter of shame for either.

Miriam did not lord her new status over the other women: she was not the type to do so. If she had been, she would not have had that status to lord with. She shared their chores as she had always done; slept with them in their tent when she was not with Yeshua. The women did not hate her. They were glad for her and glad for Yeshua. They might have wished they too could have him, but they were content that he had her comfort.

The men did not mind either. Yeshua might be more open to women than other holy men, indeed other non-holy men; the disciples might have absorbed some of that attitude from him; but they were still men of their time and place. Women did not matter enough for the men to worry about them, except that they performed their roles of wives, mothers, servants and companions. If they had been rigorous in their sexual morals they would have looked askance at Miriam's place in their band: while she and Yeshua lived together somewhat like wife and husband, there had been no formal ceremony uniting them, bar the most ancient one of all: a man taking a woman as his own. But men of such a mindset would not have joined Yeshua as his disciples in the first place. In any case, they were pleased with Yeshua's relaxed attitudes to sexual adventures within their band, and not hypocritical enough to complain if Yeshua himself did something similar.

Yehuda was accepted too, but there was an unstated distance

between him and the others. Perhaps it was because he was not a Galilean. Though Magdala was in Galilee and he had lived there for several years, Kerioth lay in a different region, south of Jerusalem. Perhaps it was simply that he held himself apart, often taking himself some distance from camp to stare into the distance and the sky. Yet the others knew that despite his distance from them he was closest of them all to Yeshua, a friend from his boyhood and a man whom Yeshua clearly held dear.

Perhaps that was part of the reason too. Chief among the disciples was Shimon known as Kephas, the Rock. He was a large, bold, outgoing man of great passions: whether the situation called for fear, anger or laughter, Shimon Kephas would respond liberally. Yehuda was a man of quieter outward passions and more intense mind; the two would never be good friends. Privately, he thought Shimon's nickname referred to the substance between his ears. The two treated each other civilly but there was a coolness between them. How much of that was because Kephas was jealous of Yehuda's closeness to Yeshua was never admitted by Kephas, especially to himself.

"I do not like that man," Kephas confided to his brother Andreas, one night shortly after Yehuda and Miriam had joined their group. "His mind is too quick; such men are sly and cannot be trusted. And have you noticed? He joined us in Magdala, the same day Miriam came to us. Have you seen that she will not look at him? It must be he who lay with her. He followed her here, perhaps to enjoy more of her charms! But she is wise and will have nothing to do with him. So not only is he sly, he is a coward, a liar and a betrayer. And he carries a *sicara*, the weapon of an assassin, who does not fight men honestly but comes to them like a thief. I do not know why Yeshua accepts his presence."

"She was found in adultery, and Yeshua forgave her. Perhaps he forgives Yehuda as well."

"Miriam does not."

"Which of us is Yeshua's equal in wisdom or forgiveness of sins? Do you think a mere woman, especially in such circumstances, would be?"

"I just hope Yeshua knows what he is doing, and is not blinded by his youthful friendship with the man."

"Have you ever known Yeshua to be blinded by anything?"

"No. But he is just a man. For all his wisdom: he is but a man."

"If it worries you, ask Yeshua. You know we can ask him all things."

Kephas nodded. "Then I shall."

And so Kephas, being Kephas, did. Soon thereafter he sought Yeshua out and called to him. "Yeshua, I would speak to you alone."

"Come."

When they were some distance away they sat, and Yeshua looked at him, waiting.

"Lord, I am the first of your disciples, and you know I love you. I would fight by your side though the armies of Rome and Hell itself opposed us. You know I would not ask this lightly."

"Speak, Kephas."

"I fear Yehuda, and that your memory of your friendship has blinded you to his danger. Forgive me, Lord; but you only knew him two days then. He is a liar and a coward, a betrayer."

Kephas looked at Yeshua nervously, wondering if Yeshua would respond with anger at his impertinence. But Yeshua answered him calmly.

"Shimon my friend, do not concern yourself with Yehuda. You have your role to play in what will come, as does he. Do not concern yourself with betrayals. Nothing can stop the will of the Lord our God."

~~~

Yeshua's words silenced Shimon's complaints, but without silencing either his doubts or his dislike. But he tolerated Yehuda, as did the others; they all ate and laughed together; all together against the world on a mission toward a greatness hinted at but never fully revealed.

One night Miriam sought Yehuda out as he sat on his rock thinking his thoughts. She did not touch him, but for once she looked at him, and her look burned him as much as her touch would have.

"Yehuda."

"Miriam."

"Yeshua told me. You did not abandon me or betray me. I have wronged you by thinking so. Forgive me."

"It does not matter. You were right to hate me. Whatever I intended, still I abandoned you in the night to face your father's rage, alone and undefended. Still I left you to be judged by the men of the town and treated badly at their hands. Still I could find no way to save you. I would have died for you. I would have died with you. But still you would have died. It is I who came for you that night. I who

70

brought you down. I who failed you."

"If you came for me that night, I wanted you to come. I let you in: to my home, my body, my soul. I do not regret it. You gave me a gift of a passion I never knew existed. I would do it again, even if I were to die for it."

"But now you are Yeshua's. You loved me; now you love him. It is well. He is the better man. He saved you where I could not; forgave you for the sin I caused you to do; delivered you from the agony to which I had condemned you."

"Yehuda! Yes, I loved you. And then I hated you. And yes, I love Yeshua, as much as a woman can love a man. But do you not understand? I still love you too. Do you know why I sit here and speak to you, and do not touch you? If I should reach out and touch you, the demons would come again to claim me. Love for Yeshua or no, I would... I would... well, you know it."

"But it cannot be. We both love Yeshua. Neither of us would betray him."

"It cannot be. I am sorry, Yehuda; sorry to the depths of my heart. But you had to know. I had to redeem our love, even if we may never express it again."

"I understand. I thank you, Miriam. If I must bear pain, it is pain of my own cause and choosing. Now go. I love you; I may always love you. But go. Go to your true love, a man greater than us both."

"Goodbye, Yehuda of Kerioth."

He watched her go, remembering the first time he had watched her walk away from him; his heart now burning with an emotion he dared not identify or name.

CHAPTER 12: THE MIRACLE OF THE WINE

Of all the disciples the one Yehuda was closest to was Teoma, the Twin. He shared Yehuda's native cynicism, but followed Yeshua loyally because he too had seen something in him which spoke not only of greatness but of goodness. And like Yehuda his cynicism increased the more self-important and self-righteous a man was; such sins were not to be seen in Yeshua.

"You know, Yehuda, many of our friends here begin to think Yeshua is the Messiah," he said one night. "What do you think?"

"I know only that he is wise and has the mark of greatness upon him. But he carries no sword and leads no army, so how can he be the Messiah? I follow him because he is my friend, and because he has done a good thing past repaying. And you, Teoma?"

"I shall follow him wherever he goes. But I do not know where that is."

He paused, looking into his wine.

"You know our lord Yeshua has done many miracles. See this wine," he continued, possibly after having imbibed too much of it: "Did you know that before you joined us, at a wedding in Cana, Yeshua turned water into wine? The story is quite famous. You should ask Yeshua about it one day."

"You were there? What do you say?"

"I saw it. Yet what I saw might not be what the tales say."

But he would say no more.

Yehuda thought about this, thought about other things he had seen, and one night approached Yeshua alone.

"Yeshua, I need to understand."

"Speak."

"The day you saved Miriam's life, you know I saw it. But what I also saw disturbs me."

Yeshua just gazed at him with his perceptive eyes, as if waiting for him to name the words he already knew.

"They said she was possessed by demons. You had her stand, and did touch her on the forehead. Then she fell with a cry; and you said the demons had left her."

"It is so."

"Yet she was possessed by no demon. She believes she was, for she cannot understand how else she fell so far so fast otherwise. But there was no demon. There were only my eyes and the desires of our flesh. If she was indeed possessed by demons you did not cast them out: the demon is me, and among your disciples is a devil."

Then Yeshua laughed, and for a moment it was if Yehuda was seeing the laughing face of a boy, a boy sitting back in the dust of a Jerusalem street.

"Oh Yehuda, wisest of my disciples! Hold out your hand."

Yehuda did so, puzzled. Then Yeshua placed his over it, looked him in the eyes, then without apparent movement Yehuda's hand was jerked downward with surprising force. Yehuda looked at it, surprised.

"Now consider a woman: hungry, terrified, beaten, in fear of her life. She is made to stand before her accusers and a holy man who, given her grievous sin, she could expect to condemn her very name to Hell before himself casting the first stone into her face. He places his hand on her forehead, gently pushing her back onto her heels and more; then what you just felt in your own flesh is applied to her forehead. What woman would not then fall to the ground, and cry out? What man would not?"

Yehuda looked at him, not fully understanding; not willing to believe what these words must mean. Not willing to ask or name it, instead he asked another question. "Teoma said you once turned water into wine but it too was not what it seemed. I myself have seen the sick cured by your passing. What do you say of that?"

"Hear me, Yehuda. Hear and understand. For if you understand this you will understand the Kingdom of Heaven. Do you think one day I put down my hammer and my saw, went out into the world and began to preach? That Yeshua the Prophet just appeared in the world, as the Greeks say their Athena appeared fully formed out of the head of their false god Zeus? No. When I knew my calling I went to study with the hermits, the holy men and the ascetics; finally the great Baptist himself. Many of these men need signs and wonders to show the people they are from God. But the Lord will not be tested or commanded. Miracles may not be forthcoming. They know the ways to ease them into being.

"I tell you, Yehuda. Some of those men are plain charlatans: they do their tricks to gain the praise of men or gruel for their bowls. Some of their tricks a fool should see through. But the best of them are artists; some even believe that what their own skill achieves is truly a miracle granted by the Lord."

"But what trick can turn water into wine, enough for a whole wedding, of enough quantity and quality to impress even the steward? What tricks can cure the lame and the blind?"

"Yehuda, first you need to understand men. They hear what they want to hear; they believe what they want to believe; and they relate tales to their own glory as much as that of the man they praise. If I turn water to wine and give it to one man in the presence of several, he will be amazed; they will taste it and they too will be amazed. They will tell the story to others. They in their turn will add their own details, to make their tale more dramatic, often believing it must be so. If men want to believe enough, it will not be long before the one cup has become an amphora; before the taste of a few becomes the praise of a steward.

"It is so for all things. Feed a few in the wilderness and the tale will grow until you have fed a multitude, with more crumbs remaining than food you began with, even to the exact number of baskets they filled.

"If a man is lying in his bed, unable to walk for pain, and a holy man touches him: he may forget his pain, he may cry out in joy; he may follow the holy man down the street, dancing his praises. Or perhaps a man, his eyes fading with age, touches the robe of that holy man, and imagines that he is already seeing more keenly; that soon he will have the eyes of his youth. He also tells his tale; of how he is blessed.

"By the time the holy man reaches the next town, more often than not the tales will have preceded him. He now cures the lame; restores sight to those blind from youth. And if it was enough, and they are indeed healed: well enough. But if the man returns to his bed or his eyes dim again? Will they even say it, having declared how blessed they are by God Himself? Or if they do, how many will care to repeat it?

"Indeed, the cripple lying again in his bed may come to hear the story of the cripple who was healed, and blame himself for his own lack of faith. For surely if he had the faith of that other man, he would himself be walking straight as a youth; not knowing the tale is his own.

"Truly, you do not need to even lift the sick from their mats. Speak to a man lying gravely ill in his bed and he dies; well, that is what happens. You gave him comfort, easing his way to join his fathers: you are a good man, and it is no fault in you that he goes the way of all men. But if his illness leaves him, as it may do, and the next day he rises from his bed: then you have cured the sick. Before long, you may even have raised him from the dead, calling him out of his very tomb!

"And that is not all you need to understand about the minds of men. They imagine their memories are like proclamations carved in granite, or the mosaics on the floor of a palace. They think they can revisit them and they are as eternal as stone, unchanging from day to day and year to year. But they are wrong. Their memories are paint in the rain of their passions. In time, even those present at the event may come to believe the tales and swear to their truth."

Yehuda could only stare, appalled. "So it is a lie? It is all a lie?!"

Yeshua sighed. "A lie? I have never said anything. I merely do. What men say about it is their concern."

"You told the crowd you cast the demons out of Miriam!"

"You see, Yehuda? Even you, who knew the truth and saw the spectacle, had no eyes to see or ears to hear. I said I had the power to cast out demons by the power of the Holy Spirit. But by such power as that, who would not? Then when Miriam fell to the ground, I said only that no demons now tormented her. I never said they had. I only repeated the claims of others."

Yehuda gazed at him intently, seeing the shape of something, as if a barrier had been broken but he could not yet penetrate the mists beyond. "Yet you let men believe a lie."

"My friend, I said you need to understand men. You also need to understand faith. Faith does not operate out there, in the world. It will not raise stones to build a temple, or cure the sick by a word. Faith is in here!" he said, striking his chest with his fist. "In men's hearts! And in there, it can move mountains. In there, it can move men to raise stones into a temple and lift a sick man from his bed. It is there where men will find God. It is there that the Kingdom of Heaven will be built!"

Yehuda continued staring, at last beginning to see a shape forming from the mists.

"Yes, Yehuda. I do miracles, but they are not the miracles men think they see. What is out there in the world does not matter. It is a shadow. I have come not to heal their bodies but to lead their spirits to the Lord Most High. If the miracles they see are a lie, they are lies in shadows, without substance; the lies are but a means for them to know a higher truth."

"Is the world a shadow? Do the Romans not rule us with iron? Do we not have to eat and drink? Do we not lay in pleasure with our women?"

"Do not mistake me, Yehuda. Yes, the world out there is real: for did not our Father in Heaven create it for us? But men have been sowing their grain, catching their fish, drinking their wine and taking women to wife since Adam left the Garden, and they will continue to do so even to the end of the world. They do not need our help for that. We do not need to concern ourselves with their bodies: for that they have sufficient concern of their own. It is in their souls that they are lost. It is their souls I have come to save."

CHAPTER 13: FISHERS OF MEN

Cynics rarely think of themselves as cynics: they are merely people with a clearer vision of the foibles of men and gods. Nor do skeptics think they are overly skeptical: they too merely see more sharply than their more gullible brethren. Others have different personalities and estimations. But if Yehuda and his friend Teoma had displayed their peculiar bents from an early age, they were far from alone in that.

Shimon son of Yohanan was born in the town of Bethsaida in Galilee, and if his eyes showed an intensity to rival those of Yehuda it was an intensity focused in quite a different direction.

He looked around at the beauty of the world and saw the hand of God. He looked at human happiness and joy and saw the love of God. He saw human sorrow and saw the stern hand of God. He gazed upon the might of Rome as it cast its long shadow over his homeland, and he saw the mystery of God.

He believed in the God of his Fathers with the absolute faith of one who held not even the conception of doubt. For how could one doubt what was visible all around you? Yet his heart held a yearning, and he knew not what it was for.

One day, when he was fourteen, his older brother Andreas told him of a preacher in the wilderness. "Some whisper," whispered Andreas, "that this man is the Messiah!"

Shimon's pulse quickened at this news and he asked eagerly, "Do you think he is? Andreas! Do you think he is?"

But Andreas just smiled. "Who can say? If he is, we will learn soon enough."

The man was not the Messiah. His fame passed as quickly as it had arisen, and his name was soon forgotten among the people of Galilee.

But Shimon had discovered the meaning of his yearning.

One day I shall find the true Messiah, and follow him to glory.

His brother Andreas was also a man of faith, though few including him could muster as much faith as Shimon. He was also a young man, no longer a boy but still not having seen his twentieth year. The idea of a Messiah, a King who would free his people, filled him with excitement too.

But no more Messiahs came near, and the boys became men. They married, as most men did; and moving to nearby Capernaum began their adult lives as most men did, doing the profession of their father. They were fishermen, for the Sea of Galilee was replete with fish.

It was a profitable life, but a hard one and not without its dangers. But men of that era were used to hardness and familiar with danger. They fed well, their wives and children fed well, and they were happy.

One day they were fishing near the shore. It had been a poor night for them, and they stayed fishing more in stubbornness than in hope. Many times more they cast their nets, and many times more the nets came up empty. The sun was becoming hot and their tempers hot too.

They noticed a man standing alone on the shore: watching them. He stood still, with the air of a man who had waited a long time. When they looked up at him he cried out to them, "What are you doing?"

"We are fishing!"

"It does not appear so!"

"We do not need strangers to tell us our business! We are busy! Leave us!"

"But I would see you fish."

"And I would see you go!"

"Cast your nets into the water on the other side of your boat!"

"If we do, will you go away?"

"I will go away."

And so they cast their nets on the other side, and this time they came up with many fish. Amazed, they pulled their catch into their boat and went to shore near the man.

"Who are you, oh King of the Fishes?" asked Shimon.

"I am Yeshua of Nazareth."

"Yeshua of Nazareth? Are you not the teacher? I have heard men speak of you."

"And what do they say?"

"Some whisper," replied Shimon in an echo of that long ago conversation, "that you are the Messiah."

"Then do not cast your nets for mere fish. Come with me, and I will make you fishers of men."

The two looked at each other, both thinking they should laugh out loud at his outrageous request. They were grown men with families and a livelihood. But as they looked at each other their grins vanished, as the siren song of the Messiah called to them across the years Shimon had invoked.

"Then I shall follow you," said Shimon.

Andreas was older, wiser and more cautious. "Little brother," he admonished, though in truth Shimon had grown to be larger than he, "you were always impetuous. For once think before you act. What of our families, our boats? We do not even know this man is the Messiah."

"Do what you will, Andreas. I have seen; I believe. Others can look after our boats. Our mouths will not be here to be fed and our portion can go to them, along with some of the excess."

Andreas was going to object. But the siren call had him too, and when he looked into the dark eyes of the teacher he saw a wisdom he could not fathom and a command he could not deny.

"Well, someone has to look after you, little brother. Teacher, to you I give my heart and my arm, and I shall follow you wherever you go."

~~~

These were not the first men who had followed Yeshua, nor would they be the last. But most of the others formed a shifting tail behind the comet that was Yeshua of Nazareth. They saw and were amazed. They were struck and followed. Then the necessities of life, or a yearning for their families, or one of the many other pressures or disillusionments men were prone to, saw them leave. Some would return, if only when Yeshua returned to their region and they could watch and hear and learn without excessive inconvenience. Few would forget their time with him, for few could not be struck with a mark that would never leave them.

But most saw and followed. Shimon and Andreas were the first he called to himself. They were not the last. Soon after that he called another two brothers fishing the Sea of Galilee, Yaakov and Yohanan the sons of Zebediah. Then as Yeshua's fame and travels grew, he chose more.

Shimon did not mind. There was room for hundreds in Yeshua's heart and circle; thousands. But he knew from the moment he gave his heart to Yeshua that he would be his right hand man; he had known it since he was a boy of fourteen. Yeshua saw in him a great strength, and named him Kephas, the Rock. For his heart was great in more than faith: he was loyal, impetuous, commanding and bold. There was no room in it for the lesser emotions of doubt or jealousy.

Except for one man. Shimon never understood why Yeshua had chosen Yehuda to be one of the Twelve. All the others were from Galilee, Yeshua's own home region, and though Yehuda had joined Yeshua in the Galilean town of Magdala he had come from Kerioth, in the south of Judea. That also Shimon did not mind. There was room in Yeshua's teaching for the whole world. But Yehuda had not been called like the others. He had simply come, and then under suspicious circumstances.

Miriam would not speak of it, but Shimon was convinced that he was the man who had betrayed her. And the man thought too much. Often when they camped in the wilderness Shimon would see him, away from the others, casting rocks and his unspoken thoughts into the darkness. The darkness was not only beyond. There was a darkness in him, a darkness Shimon could neither understand nor penetrate. When Shimon looked at Yeshua he saw a shining light; the Hope of Israel. When he looked at the others he saw lesser lights, men like him, flawed but sincere; men he could trust with his life. But when he looked at Yehuda all he saw was a shadow, and he wondered what that shadow hid.

He knew that Yehuda was uncommonly clever, but that meant nothing to a man like Shimon. Cleverness was a distraction and a snare; men who thought too much doubted too much and plotted too many of their own plans. Yeshua was different. He was not clever. He was beyond clever. His genius was like the Word of God brought into human form, a genius to be admired: something that could not be questioned, only faced and worshipped like a flower to the sun.

Yet Yeshua not only accepted Yehuda, but was perhaps closer to him than to all the others: even Shimon whom he loved like a brother, even Yohanan whom he loved like a son. But the only mark of distinction Shimon could see in him was that he, alone among them all, had known Yeshua as a child. But that had been a matter of only a day or two; more decades ago than days together. Yet in that brief meeting a bond had been forged which would not be broken, neither by distance nor by time nor even by betrayal.

Then when Yeshua chose him as the keeper of their purse, Shimon felt he had to speak again. By the criteria of men Yehuda was not a poor choice: as a potter beholden to others he was used to the holding, recording and apportioning of coin. But surely Mattithyahu, a former tax collector, was even more qualified?

So one night Shimon sought out Yeshua to speak with him about Yehuda for a second time.

"Shimon. You are troubled."

"Yes, Lord. I know you met Yehuda as a child. But children grow into men, and sometimes what the child had the man has lost. Are two accidents of meeting enough to know a man?"

"There are no accidents, only destiny."

"But can any man, even you, Lord, know another man's destiny? I can understand your friendship, for men's friendships follow their own reasons. But I do not understand your trust in him. I see a darkness in him. Yet you chose him as one of your Twelve. Yet you trust him with our treasury."

"Those who follow me will follow me. Those whom I choose, I have chosen."

Yeshua would say no more and Shimon could make no answer, so he nodded and departed. If Yeshua had chosen Yehuda then he must be worthy. But somewhere in the darker depths of his mind his doubts of Yehuda remained, their darkness made blacker in the shadow of the absolute light of his faith.

That faith was enough for Shimon, and no doubt of a mere man could touch his faith in one who was more than a man. Then one day Yeshua was sitting with his Twelve, all relaxing in the cool of the evening.

"You have heard me call myself the Son of Man. What do others say of me?"

"Many speak of you, but none know. Some say you are Yohanan the Baptist back from the dead; others think you may be Eliyahu returned from Heaven to usher in the end times; still others say you are Yirmeyahu reborn."

"Whom do you say I am?"

The others looked at each other, uncertain what to reply. Then Shimon stood and calmly pronounced in a voice that held a certainty beyond challenge, "You are the Messiah, the Son of the living God."

"Behold Kephas! Behold my Rock!" said Yeshua, then addressed him directly.

"You are Kephas, my Rock, and upon this rock I will build my assembly, and neither man nor hell will prevail against it."

It was the proudest moment of Shimon's life, the moment for which he had been born. One day in the far future he would die, killed by men for his words and his faith. Over the years until then he would do many things he was proud of and others whose memory brought him burning shame. But on that day he would think of this moment, the instant that had defined his life, knowing the words had been true; holding its image before him like a shield as he slipped into the final darkness.

CHAPTER 14: THE WANDERERS

Whatever fates awaited the men who followed Yeshua were far into their futures. There was no room in the present for such thoughts. This was the spring of Yeshua's journey, not the autumn of their lives. These were the heady days of the excitement of the unknown and the wonder of great things to come.

In some future millennium, young men who imagine they have skills of instrument or voice will form themselves into performing bands, partly for the enjoyment they gain in the present but with the underlying hope of fame and fortune in the future: if only they could break free of the pack and have their unique talents recognized. Thousands of attractive young people will embark on acting careers with much the same motives. Whatever small successes they achieve, most will sink with little trace into the great expanse of mankind and find more prosaic methods of earning their bread.

In Roman Judaea, prophets had similar trajectories and prospects.

It was a more dangerous career, however. The crowds were fickle and could be credulous one day but demanding the next. If a prophet promised too little nobody would be interested. If he promised too much and found he could not deliver, whether in reality or perception, he could find himself in trouble. Or as Yohanan the Baptist had discovered, for all that the adulation of the crowds gave an illusion of strength, it proved without substance if one earned the ire of a king or worse, his wife.

Yeshua had something new. His disciples had seen it and followed him. The crowds saw it and adored him. And so as the weeks turned into months and the months into years, Yeshua and his band travelled around Galilee and beyond to Jerusalem itself, moving from village to village and town to town. As his fame grew so did the crowds. The more tales of miracles preceded him, the more followed in his wake. The more people talked about him, the more skeptics arose to challenge him. The more the skeptics challenged him, the more he confounded them and the higher is reputation grew.

More often than not his words were cryptic and he spoke in parables, allowing his listeners to graft their own conclusions onto his words. Thus was his wisdom apparent to all. He also taught by example. He did not merely preach that the Kingdom of Heaven was open to all including the most humble, then spend his nights in the company of rich men or scribes. He shared his meals with whomever would welcome him: rich or poor, friend or stranger, respectable or disreputable. He saw no difference between the house of a Pharisee or Sadducee and a table shared with tax collectors and prostitutes. All men were sinners: so why should he despise the one and welcome the other?

He feared no man. He accepted the rule of the Romans but did not support it. If his beliefs agreed in some ways with the scriptural strictness of the Sadducees or the more spiritual beliefs of the Pharisees, still he did not stint in his criticisms of either where he disagreed. This made the people love him the more, and if it earned the enmity of many of the ruling class, still it earned him the respect of some.

One underlying theme ran through everything Yeshua said and did: what lies in a man's heart and spirit is all that matters. The rituals and minutiae so beloved of the Pharisees were irrelevant: if a man observed every ritual to perfection yet hated his neighbor or coveted his wife, then none of his ritual purity mattered an iota. But if a man were good in his heart and spirit, it did not matter if he did not follow the rituals. The rituals were a sign, a symbol: when all God cared about, and all Yeshua cared about, was the reality. As Yeshua would say even about the Holy Sabbath day, the rituals and observances were made for man, not man for them.

And thus it did not matter if a man were rich or poor; it did not matter if you were a man or a woman; it did not matter if you were respectable or sinner, if you truly sought repentance; ultimately it did not even matter whether you were Jew, Samaritan or Gentile. If the

Jews had been God's Chosen People, still God created all men and they were all His children.

This theme was not limited to men's personal lives. It was true of the Kingdom of God itself. Many in the crowds wondered if this man was the long-awaited Messiah, come to free the Jews from their oppressors. And Yeshua spoke often of the coming Kingdom. But he did not speak of swords and armies, only of what lay within. He did not speak as if God and his army of angels would come down to Earth to scatter their enemies, but as if Man would ascend into Heaven where his enemies could not follow. The Kingdom of Heaven did not reside on Earth. It belonged in the hearts of men, and beyond the Earth.

Few understood this, least of all those who heard the rumors and not the man. If Yeshua spoke in a way to draw men's conclusions from their own hearts, then what he drew from the hearts of his enemies was also fear.

The people loved him, but that had not saved Yohanan the Baptist. Yeshua had his supporters among those of power and influence; perhaps these were men of purer heart or more flexible wisdom. But he had attacked too much of the Pharisees' source of their own pride: in their eyes he was an enemy of the true religion, and any claim by such a man to be the Messiah must be blasphemy. The Sadducees sought accommodation with Rome: they believed in their God with as much fervor as anyone else, but were more amenable to absorbing the wisdom of other races. But a claim by any man to be the Messiah would be an affront to Rome. Any move to power by such a man would be a threat to Rome that she would not tolerate.

So both groups watched nervously as Yeshua's fame grew, annoyingly immune to their criticisms and arguments. Then one year he finally made his move. As the great Feast of the Passover approached, so did Yeshua, and so did the crowds. Thus their contempt and nervousness hardened into hatred and fear. If he declared himself King the people would rise up with him, and Israel would be destroyed. If he did not, the people might declare him King regardless.

Before, he was an insult, a slap in the face, an annoyance. Now he was a deadly danger.

But Yeshua had timed his move to perfection and they had left theirs too late. If they tried to stop him now they would cause a riot: the crowds would turn on them as well as on Rome.

He had to be stopped. They just did not know how.

CHAPTER 15: JERUSALEM

The meal that night was abuzz with excited conversation. After one merry exchange, Kephas even clapped Yehuda on the shoulder in cheerful companionship. The talk was of the future, of the crowds, of triumph.

Tomorrow they would ride into Jerusalem.

This was not the first time they had come to Jerusalem in their wanderings. But this time it was different. This time there was something about the crowds: their numbers, their excitement, their anticipation. It was as if the people were waiting for something with bated breath and a song in their hearts waiting to break free.

Yeshua joined in the celebration, though giving only cryptic answers to questions about the details of what was coming. When Yehuda looked his way, more often than not Yeshua's face bore a look more of sorrow than celebration.

After their meal Yeshua left alone and went a short distance up the Mount of Olives, where he rested, meditated and prayed. He heard soft footsteps and looked up.

"Yehuda. Come, sit."

"You are troubled."

"You know why."

"I am no prophet, my friend."

"Yet you see that which others do not. You see the patterns and the shapes they foretell. Tell me, what will happen when we ride into Jerusalem?"

"Shimon Kanai believes you will declare yourself the Messiah and begin the rebellion that will cleanse our land of the Romans. Most of the others believe something similar."

Yeshua looked at Jerusalem in the distance. "And what will happen after that?"

"They believe the Lord is with you. They see the people are with you. With such power, we will overrun the garrison; having won Jerusalem, the whole country will rise up with us, and we will expel the Romans from our land."

Yeshua was silent for a long while. Finally he spoke. "The empire of Rome stretches from the rising of the sun to its setting. But even Rome is beset by enemies, strong as Rome within their own domain or Rome would own them too; forever seeking signs of weakness. Rome will not lightly bear any loss of its dominions. A hail of iron would descend upon us. We would be crushed. Within a year, perhaps two, Jerusalem would be razed, its Temple desecrated, its people put to the sword: and crucifixes would line the roads from here to Kesariya."

He looked again at Jerusalem, as if seeing the flames of its burning before his eyes; as if hearing the screams of its people within his ears; as if seeing the miles of the dead.

"The men believe you are the Messiah. You yourself have said the Kingdom of Heaven is coming. What are the Romans, against the power of the Living God?"

"Men hear, but do not understand! They look to the past, and imagine the restoration of the glory of Israel. They imagine their Messiah as another Yehuda HaMakabi, come to throw off the yoke of their oppressors." He paused, searching Yehuda's face for understanding; then he continued.

"The time for such dreams is past. The Kingdom of Heaven is not out there," he said, gesturing as if to encompass the whole world, "but in here!" he said, thumping his heart with his fist. "I have not come to replace the Emperor of Rome with a King of Israel. I have come to do away with Kings. It is not important who rules a man. It is only important how he rules himself. It is not important who he gives his taxes to, only that he gives his heart to God. We do not need to conquer Israel: for when it lives in the hearts of enough men, the Kingdom of Heaven will conquer Rome itself. You alone of my disciples truly sees this."

"Yet there is more I cannot see."

"What do you see, Yehuda? When you look at the crowds; when you look at my disciples?"

"The crowd grows in numbers and passion. They are like a pot coming to the boil. The Disciples too: their anticipation is greater, but so is their fear; both feed off the crowd. Our fellowship begins to crack. For all our joy tonight, for all that we travel together toward the same end: our sight of that end is different. There are conflicts in goals, conflicts in means, conflicts between men. I fear the next week. I fear we come to our climax, for good or ill."

"I see it too. It is like a great rock being heated in the fire. While it heats, it seems stronger: for who dares touch it? But what would happen, if that rock were plunged into cold water?"

"It would crack. Smash into fragments."

"Indeed. The time is now upon us. We have spoken of the course of holy men: how the crowd loves them, until they fail. Most fail soon: their message or signs too weak to long hold the crowd. But even Yohanan the Baptist did not achieve what we have. Tomorrow the crowds will cry out for us. The fever will take the city. They will whisper of the Messiah. Both joy and danger will stalk the city, equally deadly.

"If I declare myself the Messiah, the future of which we spoke will come to pass and ruin will come to us all. If I do not declare myself the Messiah, the crowds will turn from us, perhaps on us. My ministry will be over and my message will be lost. From such ashes of betrayed joy and hope, nothing can arise again."

Yehuda stared at him. "Then we are lost. It was all for naught."

"No. There is a third way. Remember what I told you about Akhilleus and the choice he faced? Now is the time for mine. I can do nothing; I can take Miriam and return to Nazareth, return to the trade of my father Yossef. There I can live in obscurity until I am gathered to my fathers an old man, surrounded by my children. Or I can die before the week is out, at the peak of the crowd's fervor, and usher in the Kingdom of Heaven."

"But why must you die!? Surely there is another way!"

"I have prayed to my Father in Heaven to show me one, but He is silent. Do not mistake me, Yehuda. I do not wish to die; I do not wish to die in the manner which surely faces me. I do not wish to leave Miriam; I do not wish to leave you, my dearest friend. But die I must."

"But why!?"

"The future hangs on a thread. Shimon Kephas is my rock: his faith is unshakeable, and he will follow it to Hell or Heaven. But rock is not bronze: it is strong, but it will not bend; it will bear enormous pressure, but then it will crumble. In Kephas I see a greatness, enough greatness to win the world. But he is blind. He sees only a Messiah who will free Israel. You have seen him: you have seen the look in his eyes. He sees that Messiah in me; he cannot doubt it. What will happen to him, when he reaches what he thinks he sees and finds a mirage?"

"It will destroy him."

"Yes. Not immediately, for he has great strength and will stand for a while, breaking but not yet falling: but that will only make his final fall the greater. It is up to you to save him, and to do that you must understand him. You and Teoma, your eyes are larger than your faith: you must see to believe. But Kephas' faith is larger than his eyes: he does not have to see to believe. But that strength is also his blindness, for he cannot see beyond his faith. So he must want to believe, need to believe: and you must show him what to believe. When his faith is betrayed he will begin to break; resisting it with his great heart but the pressure feeding on his own resistance. But no animal can watch itself be destroyed. If you show him the way out he will take it, as a drowning man will grasp for any support."

"But what is his way out?"

"He must learn what I have told you tonight. What I have told all of you before this, but none could understand. He must learn that the Kingdom of Heaven is not of this Earth. You all must learn it: not as words from my mouth, but as the truth in your bones."

"But…" whispered Yehuda. "But how?"

"The Son of Man must die. He must descend into Gehinnom. That is what will destroy Kephas, for it will seem to him that all he believed was a lie even his faith cannot escape. But then the Son of Man must rise again, to join his Father in Heaven. That is what will save Kephas; save you all. That will be the birth of the Kingdom of Heaven."

CHAPTER 16: A BAG OF SILVER

It was night, the time for actions like these. He moved furtively down the street, turning his face away from the few other men he encountered on their own innocent or more likely guilty missions.

When he came to the entrance flanked by torches and guards he paused. If he stepped over that threshold the die was cast. The guards looked at him suspiciously and shifted on their feet. These were dangerous times. If this man was a *Sicarius* and believed the Temple was sailing too close to Rome, he might approach in seeming innocence before plunging his blade into them as a lesson to the rest.

Perhaps the man read their minds, or their posture, for he held his hands away from his body and approached.

"I wish to see the Priests."

"Come back during the day."

"The day is not the time for things such as this. Go. Ask them if they wish to receive me. Tell them it concerns Yeshua of Nazareth. If they do not wish to see me now, they need not see me at all."

The guards looked at each other. One nodded to the other, who went inside, while the first held his weapon at the ready, barring the way. A short while later the second man returned. "The Priests will see you now."

He was escorted into their presence. No introductions were made. He knew who they were, for they were the Priests of Jerusalem. They knew who he was, for they had made it their business to know all the chief disciples of Yeshua.

"Why are you here?"

His heart was thumping and sweat pricked his skin. There was still time to back out. He could claim he was here merely to plead Yeshua's case; to argue that Yeshua was a man of peace, a danger to neither Temple nor Rome. Or that in his trusted position he could persuade Yeshua to leave the city quietly, bringing the crowds off the boil. They would probably have him beaten and thrown out onto the street, but perhaps that was preferable to what he was about to do.

Now is the time for boldness. Cast the die that brings about the Kingdom of Heaven.

"You do not dare arrest Yeshua while the multitude surrounds him singing his praises. You cannot comb Jerusalem for him either: you have nothing on him; Pilate will not give you the men to search and you cannot spare your own guards with danger all around." Then he stopped, mouth dry.

"Did you come here to tell us what we already know?" asked one harshly.

"I am with him at all times. I know where he is and where he goes. I… I can tell you when he is alone, away from the multitude who praise his name. You can take him, far from the crowds. When they see him, charged by the Priests of Jerusalem, bowed and beaten, they will see he is no King and turn against him."

The priests glanced at each other, surprised. "Why would you do this? Are you not one of the Twelve? One of his chosen ones?"

He could not tell them his true reasons. Perhaps he could claim to have lost his faith, but he thought that would smell of a trick. The look in their eyes, a mixture of eagerness and contempt, gave him his clue.

"I am a poor man. The Temple coffers are deep."

The priests glanced at each other again, this time without surprise. *Simple men, simple motives,* the glances said to each other.

"Twenty pieces of silver, half now, half on arrest."

"Forty now."

"It is unseemly to haggle over your Master. Thirty."

He nodded, and the deal was set. He was escorted out by the guard, silver now hanging in his secret pouch. Now that the deal was done he felt no guilt, only the excitement of anticipation.

Now you will play your part, Priests. You have resisted the Kingdom of Heaven, but now you will usher it in.

And so he went walking out into the night.

CHAPTER 17: THE GARDEN

They gathered together in the room. A tension stung the air, like the promise of lightning. They knew something was coming, but knew not what. They could see it in Yeshua: in the tenseness of his pose, like a pulled bow waiting to be released; in his eyes, wide and dark: they could not tell whether it was excitement or fear, but surely it must be excitement.

He had not declared himself the Messiah, though the word was heard as whispers in the crowd. Nor had he denied it. It was as if he were whipping the crowd up to a fever pitch; yet quietly, not calling for the overthrow of Sanhedrin or Rome, but not sparing them either; calling to the crowd, but not saying to what he was calling them; drawing out their passions, but not giving those passions direction. He had spoken once of his band being a stone heated in the fire; now he acted like a man lighting fires in dry scrub and calling up the wind; but would he be able to control the firestorm, or would it consume him, and possibly all Jerusalem with him?

But for now they had an evening of rest. And so they supped together, sharing their bread and wine, telling tales and singing.

"My friends!" he called once. "My disciples! It is good that you eat and drink so merrily. The Kingdom of Heaven is coming, but it is not without price. So laugh and play, for tomorrow comes the whirlwind."

Then he passed them bread and wine, saying "One day you will understand, but you will not understand tonight. The Passover is coming, and the Lamb of God must be offered up as a burnt offering to the Lord. So as we share bread and wine tonight, remember me when you share bread and wine, from this day on until you join me in my Father's kingdom."

And so they ate and drank, but did not understand. Then Yeshua stood. "Come, my friends. Come with me to the Mount of Olives. There I will pray to my Father in Heaven, and prepare myself for what is to come. Come with me, that we may be together this last night."

And so they went up to the Mount of Olives, filled with wine and weariness, forgetting his earlier words. But one of them held the words close to his mind, and understood them. *He spoke to me. The sacrifice must be made that ushers in his Kingdom. Oh Lord, who sees the hearts of all men: give me the strength to do what must be done. For as you chose your Son, so did your Son choose me.*

Yeshua led them into the garden known as Gethsemane. "Stay, my friends; my disciples," he said. "You are weary. So stay, and watch, and wait. Kephas, Yohanan, Yaakov: come with me, and watch over me as I pray."

Then he went away, and prayed in great torment. After a while he returned, to find them all asleep. Except for one; one who could not be seen; the one he knew would not be seen. He shook his head in sorrow and acceptance, then went away and prayed again. Again he returned, and again his friend was absent. Then on the third time he was back, apparently asleep with the others: but Yeshua knew he was not asleep.

Yeshua walked softly among his disciples, saying his farewells in his mind. They were men, with all the imperfections men were wont to have; but they were also his chosen ones, each chosen for some peculiar quality of strength he saw in them. Now would be the hours and days of their greatest trial. *Please Lord may I have chosen well; give them the strength to survive what I must do to them. One will break; some may break: give them the power to mend themselves, and they will become mighty.*

Then he reached down, and touched Yehuda on the shoulder. His eyes sprung open, and Yeshua could see from the look of agony in their depths that he knew what was to come.

"Yes, Yehuda, friend of my youth. Now the time has come. Do you remember? When we were boys, did I not tell you that your kiss may mark our end? That end is now. Rise, Yehuda; kiss me, as our final farewell."

Yehuda did not want to; could not want to; but nor could he refuse. So he rose, and kissed his friend on the cheek. Then past Yeshua he saw that Kephas had also woken and followed; he saw Kephas' trembling finger pointing in his direction, a look of horror in his eyes; as behind himself he heard the sound of many feet.

He spun around, and saw men in the trees; and then there was shouting, and armed men rushed toward them from all around. Yeshua grabbed Yehuda around the shoulders, looking deep into his eyes, and hissed: "Go! Go do what you must! Your time has not yet come!"

Then as Yehuda staggered uncertainly back, Yeshua calmly faced the strangers and held up his hands. Even they, rough men sent on their appointed task, had heard of this man. Even they paused.

Kephas had drawn his sword and waving it in the air cried, "Wake! Wake, Disciples! They have come for our Lord! Arise! Defend your Master!" Then to the guards he cried, "Behold the coming of the Kingdom of Heaven!"

But Yeshua put up his hand. "No! Put away your swords! My time has ended: but yours is only now beginning! Put away your swords, my friends. It is not your fates to die tonight."

The disciples looked around at the mass of men crowding into the garden and surrounding Yeshua. The wine, the night, the shouting and Yeshua's own words were too much for what courage they had remaining: they broke and ran. The last to leave was Kephas. He just stood there, mouth open, staring as if he could make his eyes see what should be seen, not what was there; just repeating over and over again, "No! No! No!" It was impossible. Yeshua was the Messiah, the Son of God. Yet here he was, taken in the night like a common thief.

~~~

The disciples had scattered into the night. All except Kephas, who followed the men who had taken Yeshua. *It is not possible! Surely fire must pour down from Heaven to consume these men, or the very Angels of God descend to save him! No! He must be waiting for his moment! Before the Sanhedrin and the High Priest himself the Glory of God will be revealed and then his Kingdom will come. Of course! They are craven, and have betrayed their oath, yet still they are the Priests of the Lord Most High. They must see it!*

He watched as the priests questioned his Lord. But Yeshua did not fight and did not call down the wrath of God. He just faced his questioners calmly and answered them in his usual cryptic manner. They chose to take his words as blasphemy. They chose to condemn him to death. They mocked him, spat on him, beat him until he staggered to his knees. But still the heavens remained closed and silent.

A great rage began to build in Kephas. It was as if all the things he had believed with the certainty of rock were vanishing like the morning mist. It was up to him. This was his test! If the Angels of the Lord would not come, Shimon Kephas would take their place. He began to reach for his sword. It seemed to him that the very Spirit of God possessed him, and he had the power to fight to his Lord's side; then surely the Angels would at last come to their aid.

But somehow Yeshua's eyes found him among the onlookers and they were like a slap of refusal. *He knows and he forbids.* It was too much for any mortal man to bear. The onlookers turned, startled, to hear one of their number wail in a screaming sob, "No! It cannot be!" then run as if pursued by all the demons of hell.

~~~

Shimon ran blindly through the night. It seemed to him that every eye saw into his soul and found it wanting; that every face refused him; that every smile mocked his folly. "I do not know him!" he shouted at uncomprehending faces. "I never knew him!" he screamed at their eyes. "I never...! I did not...! Leave me alone!" he sobbed at their smiles. Then he ran into the darkness and fell to the ground, sobbing like the Lost in the outer darkness, who can never find their way back into the light.

After minutes or hours, he looked up. If a stranger had looked into his eyes, he would have hurried on. They had the look of madness, as if two contradictory but irresistible forces had met and were crushing his mind between their demands, leaving no way out. No escape, for all eternity.

But no organism wants to die, no matter what dire straits it is plunged into, and the disintegration of a mind is a death as sure as any other. And so a way out oozed into his mind, like oil created deep in the earth by unimaginable pressures and finding its expression through whatever tiny cracks it is forced through.

If he did not think; if he only felt; then he could act. He dare not look left or right, only on the destination. Seeing would be the end of him but in acting, he could make what he needed real. Another must have betrayed his Lord. He would make that other pay.

~~~

In their triumph, the disciples had been puzzled why Yeshua had been careful that they arranged separated places to stay in case they had to scatter. But he was Yeshua, their Lord: they obeyed. When the men had come to arrest Yeshua they had been as glad of his foresight as they were ashamed of their cowardice. Now Kephas put it to use for his grim task.

First he sought out Yaakov and Yohanan. They were together, agitated and guilty but paralyzed into inaction. They were shocked at Kephas' appearance when he burst into their room, eyes wide and almost unseeing; seeing them, but as if refusing to see anything beyond his immediate needs. As if to see any more would destroy him.

"Yaakov! Come! We must avenge our Lord!"

The two glanced at each other, wondering if Kephas meant to storm the Sanhedrin itself. "What do you mean, Shimon? How can we? We are lost. We are too few. We cannot fight the Sanhedrin. We cannot fight the Romans."

"Not them! Did you not see? In the garden? Yehuda kissed Yeshua, as the men came for him! He never was really one of us, always different, always separate. And he hated Yeshua! Hated him because he took the woman Yehuda wanted for himself! He is a devil! How did they know where to find us, far from the crowds? Someone had to betray him! It had to be Yehuda!"

Yaakov and Yohanan looked at each other then uncertainly back at Kephas. "Are you sure? He is one of us! One of the Twelve!"

"Did he not also betray Miriam? Betrayal is his nature! As the scorpion cannot help but sting, Yehuda cannot help but betray those he thinks he loves!"

The two others stood, electrified. "Let us go and speak with him!"

"Not you, Yohanan! Stay here, in case others come. Yaakov is enough, for surely the Lord will give us strength for his task."

The pair ran out into the street. They knew where Yehuda would be and made their way there, slipping through the dark streets. When they found him he was not asleep, just sitting staring out into the night, as if seeking an answer to whatever darkness prowled in his own soul.

"Yehuda, we would speak to you," announced Yaakov sternly.

Yehuda looked up. The two stood above him, faces and postures as stern as Yaakov's voice. "What is there to speak of? It is over. What are you doing here, and why do you address me like judges?"

"Why did you do it?" asked Yaakov harshly.

"What is it you imagine I did?"

"You betrayed Yeshua! You! One of the Twelve!"

"Are you mad? I did not."

"You betrayed him with a kiss! Shimon saw you!"

"Shimon knows not what he saw."

"Then we shall see!" cried Kephas. He went over to Yehuda's bag, felt around in it, pulled out a leather pouch with a shout. "Look!" he said. "A bag of silver! This is why he betrayed our Master! For silver! Nothing but a handful of silver!"

The other looked at him, aghast. Shimon was shaking and crying, as if such depths of betrayal could be the end of him too.

Yehuda looked over at him also, eyes wide and dark. "What? I have never seen that silver before!"

Kephas shook it in his face, the silver jangling like an echo of his accusation. "Yet here it is! You cannot help lying, as you cannot help betraying!"

Yehuda's eyes darted quickly from face to face, fear now showing in his own; no mercy showing in theirs. "I did not! I swear!"

Yaakov spat. "How many oaths must you break tonight, traitor?" He glared at him then looked to Kephas. "What shall we do with him?"

Kephas growled then said in a voice strangled with passion, "If he felt any remorse for what he has done, he would have hung himself already. As he has not, we should help him."

"No! No, do not do this! You must not!" He sprang to his feet to run, but they were upon him. Kephas removed his *sicara,* hid it under his own tunic and held the point below Yehuda's ribs. "Walk with us, friend," he hissed, "Walk with us to the field where you will meet our God."

And so they took him, roughly marching him along the street. If anyone were to question them, they were just helping a friend home after too much wine. But none asked or cared.

They went out into a field where they found a stout tree, and there they tied a rope. "Do you know what this place is?" asked Kephas casually as he secured it. "This place is known as the Potter's Field. Appropriate, is it not, Yehuda? Perhaps you should have stayed a potter, instead of entering the business of betrayal."

Yehuda, his arms now bound with a section of the same rope, said nothing as he looked up at the gently swinging noose. *So here it ends. Oh Yeshua, how did we come to this? How did I fail you so badly?* The image of a boy's laughing face came to him across the years. *I am sorry, my friend. Now we have both failed.*

Then Kephas said to Yaakov, "Stand guard! You do not need to sully your hands with this deed. I will do what must be done."

There was a rock nearby. If Yehuda stood on the rock, the noose could be placed over his neck and he could be pushed off it, unable to reach the ground; unable to reach the rock; doomed to death by strangulation. Kephas manhandled Yehuda roughly to the rock. Yehuda knew he could not escape, not with his hands bound so tightly behind his back. But life ran strong in his veins: he could not stand by meekly and let death take him. He sprang and ran. But it was pointless. The others easily caught him and pushed him roughly to the ground, blood now pouring freely from his nose and broken lips.

"At least die like a man, traitor!" hissed Yaakov, giving him an extra kick in the kidneys for good measure. And he was again lifted by Kephas onto the rock, water flowing from his eyes and blood from his face, spattering onto the rock and ground below. *They are both mad,* he thought. *But how can I blame them? Their world has come crashing down around their ears. Yeshua, the man they loved—the man I loved—is given over to the rot of death. He said once that I would follow him. But again it is I who leads and he who follows, this time into the realm of shadows. Oh Yeshua! You put your trust in me and I have betrayed you. Truly I am damned.*

As Kephas tied the knot roughly around Yehuda's neck, Yehuda saw the wild look in his eyes: a look of madness barely held in check, and he realized that it was as Yeshua had predicted. His faith, so rigid and unyielding, had reached a crisis it could not bear. Where a lesser man would have bent, Shimon had cracked, and his mind was cracking with it. Then Yeshua saw something else in those eyes: as if some fragment of sanity or justice remained to desperately balance the ledger of his act.

Kephas said nothing. The only outward effect of whatever lay in his eyes was a febrile tremble in his hands and arms; and a knot looser than it might have been. But then it broke out of him; Yehuda was not even sure he had intended to speak. "Go to God, Yehuda. Or perhaps our God will save you. As my fate is in His hands, now yours is also."

He stared into Yehuda's face as he teetered on his rock. Yehuda could have easily balanced on that rock were he free: but not knowing what would happen should he fall. The ray of sanity in Kephas' eyes now looked like pleading, as if seeking forgiveness and imagining that Yehuda could grant it. Or perhaps it was just the madness, for his eyes shuttered again. Reaching below his tunic, he withdrew the bag of silver coins and shook it in Yehuda's face.

"Behold your silver, traitor!" he snarled. "Spend it well in Hell!"

With that he hurled the bag to the ground so hard it burst, the coins scattering and tinkling among the rocks.

Kephas held out his hand in silent command to Yaakov. Whatever grim bond held them to their task was enough for Yaakov to understand, and he handed the *sicara* to him. Then Kephas stepped behind Yehuda and poked the point of the blade into his back below his ribs.

"It would not be seemly for one of the Twelve to execute another, not matter what his deeds," he said in something that could have been a purr or a snarl. "Much better that you redeem yourself to that small extent, my friend, by having the decency to hang yourself."

"Kephas! I beg you! Do not do this!" he pleaded, clenching his toes as if to fuse them to the rock.

Kephas whispered in his ear. "Choose, my friend. Hang yourself and perhaps the Lord God will have mercy on you. For if you do not, I can not!"

Yehuda looked around desperately but saw no mercy in their faces, just madness and condemnation. Lifting his eyes to heaven, he whispered a prayer, *Lord, I commend myself to your mercy*, and pushed himself from the rock. This would be no quick death from a broken neck, but the slow doom of strangulation. Yehuda clenched his neck and looked at the men as he swung gently from the tree.

They looked back as he hung twitching, desperately and inadequately forcing some air into his lungs. He looked down. *A mere forearm's length to the ground and safety. But a distance too far to travel.*

A howl from nearby chilled the air, followed by soft yaps and growls. "Wild dogs," said Kephas, looking toward the sound but able to see nothing. He hurled the *sicara* in their general direction but the only sound was the clang of its final bounce. Then he said, "Come, Yaakov. Justice is done. Let us go and tell the others."

So with a last look, they departed.

~~~

But when they returned with some of the other disciples, there was nothing there but the ragged and bloodied end of the rope gently swaying in the breeze, and the splatter of Yehuda's blood on the rocks below. The pieces of silver still lay scattered on the ground, some stained with blood, gleaming like an accusation and a curse.

Kephas spat on the ground. "The dogs have taken his body and have ripped his bowels open upon the earth. If the Lord was merciful he was already dead. In any case it is well."

Then they left the scene as they had found it. Kephas took one last look behind as he departed. He did not understand the tears in his eyes.

Chapter 18: Trials and Tribulations

A man sat on his rooftop garden. He had had a restless night and had woken early, and now he sat in the cool of the morning, occasionally pecking at the delicacies laid on a silver tray before him.

A low sun cast its pale pink and gold onto the walls within the city, giving them a blush of promise. It was the sort of scene that an artist would delight to paint or a poet would swoon over dramatically, and the man looked at it in civilized contemplation.

What a pesthole, he thought. *I hate this Jupiter-damned place.*

He had not started out hating the place. Many who sought rule in the far flung provinces of the Empire had a Roman arrogance that regarded the natives as barely human: human enough to screw, but otherwise not much better than a fine donkey or ox, or some other beast that could be worked until its usefulness was ended. But he regarded himself as a thinker, a man with finer sensibilities when it came to the rich tapestry of human experience and exotic cultures. *More fool me.*

Most of his fellows looked upon their posts as a handy way to loot the populace to just before the point where the populace started to squeal. Those of more greed or less sense crossed that line, and could well find themselves with a rebellion on their hands or worse, recalled by the Emperor in disgrace.

He himself was not averse to extracting gold from the natives. But he would never think of it as looting. The Empire required its due; its representatives deserved their own reward for their labors. And yes, nobody liked paying taxes, not even the Romans. But he, like most men, had a high opinion of his own culture, and didn't think the natives had much to really complain about. The Empire of Rome ruled with iron and extracted gold, but it also gave. In his view the civilization Rome brought to distant barbarian lands more than compensated for the gold she removed in the process. And complain as they might about rule from Rome, somebody was going to rule them and tax them. And complain as they might about the legions of Rome, if not for those legions somebody else would be trying to kill them. All in all, he staunchly believed, Rome was good for the world it controlled; and more people lived to die in their beds surrounded by their children than otherwise might have.

He was probably right.

But more important than gold was honor. The right man doing the right job in the right place could earn that man notice at home, even the favor of the Emperor himself, and it could be a ladder to greatness in Rome itself. He was young and proud enough to believe he was the right man doing the right job, but he cursed his luck when it came to the place.

He thought of the dreams he had had before he came here. Dreams not only of wealth and glory, but of wealth and glory obtained by ruling wisely and well, over a people who would respond to that wisdom with the gratitude of sensible men.

Now my name will be forgotten within a generation. If in some far future a man should stumble upon a stone with my name on it, he will not say to his son, 'Behold, the name of a great man of Rome!' He will say, 'Who in Hades was Pontius Pilate?'

It wasn't that Judea was poor. There were better provinces with larger honey jars to put one's hands in, but there were also worse places. It wasn't that the natives were particularly warlike or prone, or at least able, to murder innocent Prefects in their beds or as they travelled. *But they are all mad!*

He was not a deeply religious man. The gods had to be honored, of course: to fail in that duty was likely to prove as fatal as failing to honor the Emperor. But by and large the Romans were happy to honor gods from other lands as well as their own. The Egyptian goddess Isis over the years had many temples built in the Empire, even in Rome herself until Emperor Tiberius had taken a personal dislike to Egyptian deities. Even strange mystery cults were tolerated as long as their members gave proper deference to the civil religion. And that was within the city of Rome: throughout her empire, local religions were rarely suppressed. Why would they be? The world was big enough for many gods.

But these Jews! What is wrong with these people?

He shook his head at the bizarre notion of only one god. But that was just the start: from there it rolled rapidly downhill into the pit of lunacy. They weren't content to just have their own singular God: they insisted that everyone else's were false gods. What passed for a sophisticate in this blighted place would say the other gods were imaginary; the rest of them from priests to peasants damned them as evil. Where the finest artists of other races strove to honor their gods with magnificent statues, the Jews regarded that as a sin worse than murder! And objected to anyone else bringing images of their own gods into their God-damned city! And half the foods in the world were forbidden to them!

He shook his head again in despair. *What kind of God is this? He created the world in six days, his might and wisdom are unsurpassed: but he is so sensitive you can't even draw his image or speak his name, and so petty he's partial to smiting you for eating an oyster.*

For all that Rome desired to rule the world and feed upon its wealth, at least if you paid her reasonable taxes and obeyed her reasonable laws she left you alone to think your own thoughts and worship your own gods. The world, he thought, ought to be thankful that Rome was born into her religion and not this one. He shuddered at the thought of a world ruled by a Rome under the sway of this insanity. *They'd be crucifying each other over every little doctrinal disagreement when nobody else can even tell the difference! There would be civil war, not over who rules Rome but who believes what bit of nonsense!*

He shook his head sadly. *Thank all the gods that would never happen.*

He sighed. *I wonder what they will come up with to torment me today.* It was Passover time, one of their holiest feasts. Like most things about their peculiar religion he found it hard to understand. Apparently it celebrated some ancient event in which their god murdered everyone else's firstborn sons but spared theirs if they put some blood on their door. *Even Jupiter, who would turn himself into a swan to screw some girl, was never that crazy. Maybe you need other gods beside yourself so there's someone around who can knock some sense into you if you go too far.*

Crazy or not, it was an important festival, so the Prefect had to be here and he'd come up from his usual residence in Caesarea. It was not only to show honorable respect to the local people and leaders, but the holier the event the more likely trouble was. It would be bad tactics, and bad for his career, if trouble broke out and he was not here in person to crush it. For similar reasons the Tetrarch of Galilee, Herod Antipas, was also here. Pilate did not particularly like the man, but at least he was sophisticated enough to engage in a conversation without Pilate wanting to bang his, or his own, head into a wall.

Well, let's see what excitements happen in Jerusalem today. With any luck it will be just another day in just another year, soon to be forgotten except in some dusty archive nobody will ever read.

~~~

Pilate looked over the list an attendant had handed to him. Nothing exceptional. Crosses would line the skyline tonight in a grim celebration of Passover. *If the men crucified are unpopular the crowd will be entertained. If they are popular the crowd will learn to fear the power of Rome. It is a win for all concerned. Well, except for the men on the crosses.*

He saw that his presence was requested outside. *Here we go again. Merely entering my palace will make them unclean. The omnipotent God of Trivia smites again.* He sighed, something he was doing more and more often lately. He put on his sumptuous robe and swept into the courtyard flanked by two guards, their bronze polished and their iron sharp. Other soldiers were already there, lining the walls like grim decorations.

He sat with a flourish, granting an imperial gaze to the cluster of priests and other local luminaries awaiting his arrival. His distaste was better concealed than their impatience. He wondered why what looked like half the Sanhedrin was here at this hour; what the bloodied and broken man at their feet had done to earn such unusual displeasure.

"Speak! What have we here?"

The High Priest himself, one Caiaphas, stepped forward. "This man stirs up the crowds and speaks against Rome."

Pilate studied them through narrowed eyes. *Sure, and you are such great friends of Rome. What has he really done?* He looked at the man, who now stood watching him. Pilate shivered at that look, which looked like calm but wasn't: like the still feel in the air before a great storm. But the man made no answer to the accusations.

"Who is this man? What has he done?"

"Yeshua, of Nazareth. He has been wandering the country for years stirring up trouble. Now he comes to Jerusalem and the crowds welcome him like a conqueror. He claims to be King of the Jews.

Therefore he must die."

"He must die because he threatens Rome—or is it just you he threatens?"

"He is dangerous! To Rome!"

"What do you say to these charges, Yeshua of Nazareth?" he demanded. But Yeshua merely looked at him.

Pilate glared back. Could this man not have understood? The conversation had been in Greek, the common language used throughout the Empire, even here. He ground his teeth.

"Do you not understand simple Greek, man? Or do you refuse to hear any words not in your own tongue? Well you won't hear them from me!"

"You will do what you must do. Words will not change it."

Pilate was about to deliver a stinging response when he paused. There was something about this man: an intensity that looked like madness but wasn't, a dignity that was almost regal. *This is no ordinary man. Perhaps the priests are right to fear him.* But his curiosity was piqued.

"Bring him!" he commanded some soldiers. "Bring him inside, where I might question him myself. And you! Fetch Herod! This man is from Galilee—let us hear what Herod has to say."

Then Pilate went inside and sat in his meeting hall, Herod standing by his side. Yeshua was brought in and unceremoniously thrown to the floor at their feet. He looked up at them, still remaining silent.

"So, Herod, what should we do with this Yeshua of Nazareth? The Sanhedrin wish him dead, though I can only think their reasons are more to do with their own power than ours."

Herod examined Yeshua keenly. "Yes, I have heard of this Yeshua. We have all kinds of ascetics and holy men wandering around and we rarely need to kill them. This one is far more notorious than most. It is said he performs miracles: healing the blind and lame, walking on water, even calling the dead from their tombs!"

He addressed Yeshua. "Show us a sign, King of the Jews. Stand and show us your power. Make us tremble before your God! If you are from God, let God show it: then to honor Him we may let you go. If your signs are mighty enough, perhaps we ourselves must bow before you!"

Yeshua rose to his feet, for long seconds studying them but saying nothing. Finally he replied quietly, "What I have done, I have done. If it is not enough, nothing is enough."

"Pah!" exclaimed Herod, folding his arms and turning his back. "See? He is nothing. If he will not show us his power to save himself, then he has no power! He is wasting our time! Flog him and let him go. I will have nothing more to do with him!" But whether he had turned away out of contempt or to escape the dissecting gaze of those eyes, he could not admit even to himself.

"So," said Pilate, addressing Yeshua. "If you will not show us your miracles, at least answer our questions. Why do your own people want you dead?"

"They fear me."

"Ah! An answer! But look at you! You have no power! How can they fear you?"

"They fear my words."

"Is that all you have? Words? Do you speak against Rome?"

"Rome does not matter."

"You say Rome does not matter, you who stand here in her power? Why? Are you mightier than Rome? Are you the King of the Jews?"

"If you say."

"What kind of answer is that?!" he snapped. "Do you *want* to die? Why do your own people hate you so, King of the Jews?"

"My kingdom is not of this world. All I have done is say the truth. As the truth slew Yohanan the Baptizer," he added, piercing Herod's back with his gaze, "perhaps it will slay me also."

"But what is truth?" sighed Pilate.

Yeshua did not reply, but Pilate felt the intensity of his gaze like a slap which said, *You know it.*

"Take him outside!" Pilate snapped to the soldiers, as he rose and marched back out to the priests.

"I find nothing wrong with the man! Or nothing that isn't wrong with all of you!" he growled. "I shall have him flogged, and let him go!"

"No! You must crucify him!"

"Do you presume to tell me what to do, Priest?" Pilate asked thinly.

"We serve Rome! He is an enemy of Rome!"

Pilate sighed. "Well, he is your King and you claim to speak for your people. Let us ask them!"

And so he went out to address the crowd, who had gathered at the news of Yeshua's arrest and trial.

"People of Jerusalem!" he shouted. "Behold your King! Mere days ago you sang him into your city! Now your own leaders want him crucified! Hear me! Today in honor of your God and your Passover I shall also pass one over and deliver him from death! I shall release one prisoner to you! Shall I release Yeshua of Nazareth, or do you want another?"

The priests and scribes had been agitating the crowd. The crowd had loved Yeshua but then he had failed them spectacularly. Those who cried "Release him!" were drowned out by the much greater numbers calling "Crucify him!"

"He is your King! Will you crucify your King?"

"Our King is Caesar! Crucify him!"

Then a lone voice cried out, "Release Barabbas!" and it was enough. The crowd took up the chant. Yeshua had failed them; let him die. At least Barabbas, a notorious robber, fought against the Romans.

If I release Yeshua there will be a riot. If I release him, no doubt the Sanhedrin will accuse me of treason against the Emperor. But he is innocent: and instead they demand I release an actual enemy of Rome. But what choice do I have?

He looked at the crowd in angry contempt, though as much for his own helplessness as for their madness. He looked again at Yeshua, the man who wanted to die for his 'truth', whatever in Hades he meant by that.

They are all mad. Every last crazy one of them.

"Very well! Be it on your heads as his blood is on your hands! He will be crucified as the King of the Jews. So behold your King as he dies on your cross, and weep for yourselves and your children!"

With that, he spun on his heel and marched back inside. "Flog him!" he ordered the guards, "And release Barabbas! Next time make sure he doesn't make it to Jerusalem!"

And so Yeshua was flogged near to death; but even the sight of that did not slake the crowd's bloodlust or their cries for crucifixion. If anything, the sight of his humiliation increased their rage, as if his humiliation was their own and every strike of the lash was an outrage in their own flesh. Then the soldiers took him away to join the rest of the condemned.

CHAPTER 19: RESURRECTION

Miriam had been in the garden with the others when the soldiers came for Yeshua. She had cried and pleaded, but it was if the men could not see her; they did not even bother to push her to the ground: just elbowed her out of the way with the minimum force required as if making their way through reeds. She saw Kephas, a wild look in his eyes, trail the crowd. But she did not follow along, much as her heart both yearned and dreaded to see what would happen. She had to obey Yeshua's last will, even if she did not understand it.

~~~

They had lain together, she and Yeshua, on the previous night. Then, as now, she knew it would be their last time, while desperately hoping it was not.

Afterwards he had held her, gently twining her hair around his fingers.

"Miriam," he had said, "Miriam, my love of this world: I cannot bear to leave you, but leave you I must. Do not cry. What we had, what we have, can never be taken from us."

She did not argue, just wept in his arms. He would not say it, if it were not true. He would not allow it, if any power in Heaven or Earth could prevent it.

"There is one other I love. You know who he is. When I am lost, when the Disciples are scattered, you must follow him. He knows what to do and will need your help. It will be too much for you to bear if I tell you now; it will be too much to bear then. But between the two of you, the two I love most on this earth, I pray you will have the strength to do what you must."

He was silent, then, silent for a long time; and she just held him, feeling his heartbeat; wondering whether he was comforting her or her, him. Finally he spoke again, in words so rough they seemed ripped from his heart.

"Oh Miriam! Do even I have the strength to do this? Say the word! Say the word and I will betray myself. Leave, tonight! Go back to Galilee! There we can marry, live our quiet lives, and raise our children! Save me! Save us! Let the world save itself!"

"Ohhhhh.... my love!" she sighed in despair. "There is no word I would rather say. Nothing on this Earth I want more dearly. But it is the one word I cannot say." She lifted herself onto her elbow, and looked deep into his eyes; then she looked away and fell back, fearing she would fall into those eyes; fearing she would say the word after all, anything so that she may continue to look into those eyes, night after night to eternity.

"Yeshua. Yeshua! What you are is why I love you. You can no more become a normal man than you can choose to stop breathing. If I said the word I would lose you anyway. You are what you are and must do what you must do: as must we all. I do not know what terrible fate has been laid upon you or why: all I know is that you will follow it to Hell and back if you have to, and I have neither the power nor the right to stand in your way."

And then he had shut his eyes tight, and held her close; and so they remained until morning.

~~~

The men in the garden might not have seen her but Miriam well knew that would not be true of all men. She dressed herself in old clothes, put dirt on her face and covered her mouth with a rag and her hair with a cowl; then she limped hunched through the streets, like an old crone who had nothing to fear from men because she had nothing of interest or use to them.

But she carried her knife, in case further persuasion was required.

She made her way to near where Yehuda would be holed up, wondering why of all his disciples Yeshua had chosen him to be alone this grim night. Perhaps it had something to do with his mysterious mission. She would not go to him yet; not tonight, not the night of her Lord's betrayal. It would be too raw for both of them. So she sat nearby in the shadows, watching his lodging place. She did not know what he might do or whether he might flee, and she did not want to lose him. She knew she would not sleep tonight.

Once she thought she had been discovered. She had heard running feet, then of all the people in the city Kephas appeared before her, shocked to see a woman here. He looked wild, mad, even worse than before: and she quailed at the thought of what he had seen and what it had done to him. She could not afford to be discovered or recognized. She pointed a swaddled finger at him and quavered, "You! You are one of his men! That man who was arrested! Help!"

He had looked at her, stricken; not seeing her, just seeing her accusation. "No! No! I don't know him!" he wailed, then ran staggering into the night.

Oh Shimon, great-hearted Kephas. Look what has become of you. If this is what it did to you, will any of us survive this night?

Some time later she heard more stealthy steps and was surprised to discover she had been dozing. She looked up in alarm and then curiosity. It was Kephas again, now in more possession of himself and this time with Yaakov in tow. She watched as they entered Yehuda's place, wondering what this meant. She watched as they came back out into the street, holding onto Yehuda as if walking a drunk friend home. Then as they disappeared around a corner the meaning and danger finally hit her deadened brain: she sprang to her feet in alarm and began to follow them at a safe distance.

Miriam's alarm increased as she followed them to the field; edged into panic as she saw what they were doing. Should she run to them, tell them to stop? They would not listen; they would take her back with them; all would be lost. And so she waited, watching in mounting horror as first Yehuda was tied by the neck and then suspended by it. Her feet itched to run to him, to save him, and she crept as close as she dared.

Then she sat and watched him die.

~~~

Yehuda swung gently from his tree, eyes half open upon the field that would be the last thing he would see. He wondered how long he would survive, feeling the noose slowly but inexorably tightening around his neck, feeling the pain of his suspension. He had seen hangings and knew it could take some time; knew he could extend his time by remaining calm, or accelerate his death by jerking his body around in a futile attempt to escape. He wondered which was preferable. He found it did not matter. He could not choose death, whatever its final comforts; he would cling to life until his spirit was ripped from his body.

Then he heard the faint howls again, and saw shapes darting and slinking among the rocks and scrub. The dogs were back; no doubt they had smelled his blood and fear and knew they meant an easy meal. He shivered. The curs were cowardly, afraid of men; not yet willing to risk an attack but taking his measure. But he knew that men were not safe from them. Sometimes they would take an injured man; sometimes they would even tear a condemned man from his cross. He could not raise himself high enough to escape their teeth; if he kicked at them it might hold them off for a while but it would strangle him the faster.

Lord God, have mercy. Deliver me from this fate, or at least let me die before their teeth find my flesh. Then he felt sick, sick to the stomach, at the thought: for all that his own end now rushing upon him would be terrible, Yeshua's would be even worse. *And so my life of betrayals ends in failure. Perhaps the teeth of the curs are merely a foretaste of the teeth of demons. What did Yeshua say? That the torment of the damned will burn forever? Were you speaking to me, Yeshua? Was I damned in your eyes even then?*

Then his eyes opened wide in surprise as some old crone dashed into view waving a stick, like some Fury escaped from a Greek myth, and the dogs fled.

"Grrrgrumph? Rrrummeree!" *Who are you? Help me!*

Then the woman uncovered her hair and looked at him wildly.

"Mmmrmmm! Wrrrarruudngere?" *Miriam! What are you doing here?*

~~~

Miriam had watched Kephas and Yaakov talking as Yehuda swung, willing them to go, praying that there would be some way to prevent this disaster. After what seemed like a lifetime, and she feared was for Yehuda, they had left. She gritted her teeth in frustration as they headed straight back toward her, and she pressed herself into concealment until they had passed. If they saw her they must have imagined she was just what she seemed: a sad old crone, of no concern to them.

Her blood felt like ice when she saw the dogs gathering and she ran, grabbing a stout stick off the ground as she did. Still she dared not call out and attract attention to herself, but she charged in waving her stick at the curs, hoping they would not simply turn on her. To her relief, they ran. They did not go far and might return; but they ran.

She turned to look at Yehuda's dead eyes, tears in her own. Then those dead eyes opened wide, and she knew they were not dead.

"Yehuda! You're alive!" she cried in answer to his inarticulate gurgles.

Quickly, she ran up to him, grabbed him around the legs with one arm and used all her strength to lift him as best she could, while with her other hand she pulled out her knife and began sawing at his bonds. It was difficult work, and more of his blood was added to the existing splashes below before she finally released his hands. Then she wrapped both arms around him, lifting him even higher, while he struggled for the noose around his neck. He loosened it and pulled it over his head, then the two of them collapsed in a heap on the ground, gasping.

"Miriam!" he croaked. "Thank the Lord! How did you find me?"

She sat up and managed half a smile. "You may well thank our Lord. It was Yeshua. He told me to keep an eye on you. I don't think this is what he had in mind, but it saved your life."

He touched her on the hand, "Thank you. I just wish we could save him too."

"I know. But he has chosen his path, even if I don't understand it and may never. And he wants me to help you in whatever task he gave you. So here I am."

Yehuda nodded and slowly raised himself to his feet. He extended his hand, and drew her up beside him. Then he looked at the noose still swinging gently from the branch.

"Give me your knife."

Puzzled, she handed it over, and watched as he pulled the noose down then roughly sawed through it with the knife before fraying it even more and soaking it with some of his own blood. He handed the knife back and told her, "Wait here. I won't be long."

He picked his way through the rocks; somewhere along the way he discarded the loose pieces of rope. Then he returned, bearing his *sicara*.

"This is precious to me, and might be useful. They will probably be back to admire their handiwork. It is best they think me dead. With luck they will think the dogs took me. God knows they almost did."

"But why? Why did they do this to you? And what does this mean?" she asked, pointing at the scattered pieces of silver gleaming among the rocks.

"I'll explain later. I'll explain everything later. But we have to get out of here."

He looked at her, and added softly. "You came for me. You saved me. I failed you, yet you saved me. I am ashamed. But I still love you, as I will always love you: if the love of one such as I can mean anything to one such as you."

She reached out and took his hand. "You do not need to be ashamed. I know there was no betrayal. You are a good man, Yehuda of Kerioth. Now let us go and do our Lord's work."

He raised her hand to his lips, kissed it, then let it go. "Yes. We cannot save him. But we can bring his Kingdom to Earth."

Then they walked off into the night, together.

CHAPTER 20: THE WAY OF THE CROSS

Yehuda knew their enemies would be on the lookout for Yeshua's disciples, whether in fear of a rescue attempt, terror of them whipping the crowd up into riot or insurrection even now, or simply the desire to capture and punish some of them. They had Yeshua; a few more would add spice to that long sought-after dish.

So with an exchange of silver plus his own clothes he had changed his garb to that of a far region, had trimmed his beard and hair into a different style and darkened it with kohl; rubbed red dust into his skin; wrapped cloth around part of his face. Those who knew him well might recognize him, though not instantly; to others, he would be just another unimportant onlooker in the crowd, another traveler from a distant province gawking at the show.

He looked around at the crowd in contempt. He knew what they had done. How within a span of mere days they had gone from welcoming Yeshua into Jerusalem with palm leaves and hosannas, to crying for his crucifixion. Yehuda had no idea why, but the Prefect, Pilate, had wanted to save him and offered to release him. *Yeshua said one day he would conquer Rome. Perhaps he has already started.* But the crowd had refused, had cried for his crucifixion even more stridently: and chose one Barabbas instead.

Barabbas, thought Yehuda grimly, *a robber. A man who preys on others. Fighting his own countrymen as much as he fights the Romans. Released to prey more, in place of Yeshua, when all he did was teach men to pray.* He wondered at the name and whether the father he was named for was the same Abbas whom Ananias had executed all those years ago. He wondered if Barabbas had discovered who had killed his father; if he had tracked down Ananias and slain him to avenge his father. Neither Ananias nor the hard men in his employ would have been so lethally stupid as to proclaim their deed: the bodies they left on the trees were warning enough to other robbers. But secrets found ways to reveal themselves.

Yehuda would never know. Should be ever meet this Barabbas, to ask either question would reveal knowledge that would be his own death warrant.

He looked down the street at the line of dispirited men dragging the crossbeams for their own crosses toward their deaths in the nearby hills. Among them, he knew, was Yeshua. *They say they hate the Romans and love God. Yet here they are, most of them entertained by this crime. Why am I condemned to despise crowds? Why am I condemned to watch them damn the innocent? And why am I condemned to stand and watch, unable to save those I love? And this time there is no Yeshua to appear and stun the crowd into deliverance. No man is his equal, and now even his Father in Heaven has forsaken him.*

He did not carry his *sicara* this time, having left it hidden with the rest of his goods. If he were detected with one on him that would probably get him killed. As the weapon of the *Sicarii* it would brand him as one of them, an assassin or insurgent, and this time there would be no crowd calling for his release. He would die on the spot, or quickly join the line of the damned trudging to their lonely doom.

Even if he could have risked carrying his sword he knew it would do no good. There was no chance of rescue, no avenue of escape. Not with these crowds; not with the Roman soldiers alert for trouble.

Then he saw him appear nearby, dragging his cross with the others. Yehuda marveled that he could still walk. He had been beaten, flogged, and blood encrusted his brow, but still he managed to move, step after painful step. The sight was appalling, and his legs nearly betrayed him: he jerked forward, as if to run to save his friend.

A nearby Roman guard saw the movement and eyed him suspiciously. Yehuda saw his chance, a chance he never imagined he had. He gestured toward Yeshua, who looked on the verge of collapse. The guard looked Yehuda up and down, assessing the threat. "What is your name, Jew?"

"I am… Shimon," he answered nervously, giving his father's name. "Of… of Kyrene," he added, remembering his style of dress.

The soldier took another glance at Yeshua then jerked his head toward him, his expression a mixture of contempt and distaste. "Go then. Pilate wants these scum on display for the rest of you to see, not dropping in the street for us to clean up. But mind that he doesn't or you might find yourself taking his place, Shimon of Kyrene."

He ran up to Yeshua and took the weight of the beam on his own shoulders.

"Yeshua! I am here!"

Yeshua staggered, leaning his weight on Yehuda. "Ah, my foolish friend", he breathed. "Forgive my weakness. You should not have to carry both my cross and my weight. But carry us both for a while, and we shall talk. Just let me catch my breath."

He bent over and coughed into his hands; hands that came up wet with blood. He smiled weakly, "At least I will not last long after they nail me to their tree."

Yehuda could only look away. *I cannot add my pain to his.*

For long minutes Yehuda carried the weight of his friend's cross on one shoulder and the weight of his friend's arm on the other. Yeshua walked with shoulders stooped, a broken and defeated man, his head resting wearily on Yehuda's shoulder. Or so it seemed to the crowd. But as they staggered along the dusty street, Yeshua spoke his questions into Yehuda's ear and Yehuda answered as best he could, pretending he was just a stranger forced to carry a cross and offering what comfort he could to the man who would hang from it.

"Miriam, my love: is she well? Shimon, my rock: how fares he?"

"She serves you to the end. Let me tell you what has transpired."

When he had finished, Yeshua stared at him in shock. "Oh my God," he breathed, almost collapsing despite Yehuda's support. Yehuda looked back at him, startled: he had never heard Yeshua speak in such a fashion. *But neither man nor God could blame him today.*

"No, my friend, I did not expect that," Yeshua said at last. "It could all have been undone. I would have died a fool and a failure." Then he rallied. "But it is well. Yes, very well."

"But Shimon, my Lord: he breaks. Madness grips him."

"Shimon is my Rock. But to build a temple, must not the rocks in the quarry be cracked and broken before they can be shaped into their new form? So it is with Shimon. He believes too deeply, but has set himself on the wrong course. These days will break him, and he will be reborn."

Yehuda thought, *But what if his pieces scatter before he can be reborn, and neither man nor God can put them back together?* But he saw Yeshua's eyes on the distant hill before him, and he could not say it. *Even Yeshua must have his breaking point. It is not my role to make his road harder than it is. That would be a greater betrayal than the other. Let me help you, my friend. That is all that is left to me to do.*

So instead he said, "He is like a cliff that has stood since the beginning of time, now facing forces even it cannot withstand. He will not stand much longer."

"Just a few more days, Yehuda; just a few more days. Then he will break, but he will break in the direction we have set. He just has to stand that long, and you must provide his way out. All the forces you now see destroying him will make him something great. You will see."

And you will not, my friend. At least not in this world. He looked away, that Yeshua could not see his eyes. *Coward! Can you not raise a courage to match his?* He blinked away his tears, and turned back to face his friend. Yeshua was looking at him with those eyes that missed nothing, and he reddened.

"Be not concerned, my friend," said Yeshua gently. "We are all at our breaking points: not only Shimon but you, Miriam—and me. By the grace of our Lord it shall purify us like gold from the furnace. Have faith, my friend. For that is all that is left to us: but it is enough."

Yehuda squeezed the hand on his shoulder and whispered, "Yes, my friend. Yes, I know."

Then Yeshua gripped his shoulder with a strength Yehuda thought had long since left him. "But you will remember what I told you? I know it is hard. But you understand? You will do it? You must do it!"

"I will do it, though Hell itself bars the path. Only death will stop me. There is no love nor money nor honor on Earth that can stand in my way."

Yeshua nodded, suddenly unable to speak. Again he coughed and again his hand came up bloody, and he looked up the road toward the hill. Then he gripped Yehuda's arm and whispered, "Stay with me, Yehuda. Stay with me until the end."

And so the two friends walked on together, Yeshua's head resting on Yehuda's shoulder, step after step to his grim destiny.

When finally they arrived, Yeshua sank to the ground with a sigh and Yehuda dropped the cross. In the hearing of the guards Yeshua spoke to him as to a stranger: "Bless you, Shimon of Kyrene. God go with you." But his eyes said: *You do not need to see the rest, my dearest friend.*

Remember me always as I was. Remember me as a boy in a street and a man who loved you. Go in peace, until we meet in my Father's Kingdom.

"I do my duty. Go to God." *There are no words. Goodbye, Yeshua of Nazareth. Go to your Father and be at peace. You will be with me always, to the age of the ages.*

Then he melted back into the crowds, and was gone.

CHAPTER 21: THE UNFORSAKEN

Life and pain were cheap in the ancient world, and crucifixion was a punishment for the times. Those who inflicted it cared only for its effectiveness as punishment and deterrent. The fate of those they inflicted it upon was not their concern.

And so one by one the condemned dragged their crosses to the hill; one by one the beams they held were attached to the uprights; and one by one they were nailed up by hands to the beams and by feet clasped either side of the uprights. The hill became an orchard of death, a field of ghastly trees bearing even more terrible fruit.

Above Yeshua's head they fixed a sign:

The King of the Jews

This was the crime for which the Sanhedrin and the crowd had condemned him. Pilate, in his last gesture of contempt, had slapped them in the face with it: *Behold your King! Behold the fate of all who would resist the might of Rome!*

None of Yeshua's disciples were there to observe his final hours. If Yeshua was worth crucifying then he was dangerous, and if he was dangerous then so were his men. Perhaps some viewed from distance, unseen, but none dared come close.

The women were more fortunate, if fortunate is the appropriate word for being able to view one you love dying a slow and agonizing death. As long as they did not get close enough to do something stupid, nobody cared what women did. After all, what could they do? Let them watch and cry and wail. It added to the spectacle and the deterrent.

Some of the women stayed away, unable to bear what could not be borne or changed. But some distance away a group of women stood silently, among them Shelomit and Miriam the mother of Yaakov the Lesser. Yeshua could see them and he smiled at them as if in blessing, the only thing he could now give the women whose faithful service had now brought them to this.

Away from the group one woman stood alone, swathed in black robes. The others had seen her, nodded their greetings and gestured her to join them for whatever mutual comfort could be had in such a time. She had returned their greeting but refused. They did not insist. Each would have to bear their grief in their own way. They knew hers would be the hardest.

She wondered why Yeshua appeared to be growing in her vision, as if her world were collapsing into nothing but the sight of him. Then she realized she was walking toward him, as if her body were unable to bear the distance between them.

Finally she stopped, close enough to speak to him but far enough to remain safe from everything but the occasional pointed glance. But she said nothing, just gazed at the naked body she had known so well and into the eyes that had seen into her soul and possessed it.

"Miriam," he said, the word rough and torn. "I said that I would love you until the day I died, and it was true. But that day is here, and it is not enough. So hear me, Miriam: I will love you even to the age of the ages."

"And I you," she whispered.

"Now. It is set? You know what you must do? You will have the strength to do it?"

She nodded, unable to speak. *I claim the strength to act, though I have not even the strength to speak. Oh Lord, please grant me that strength when my hour comes.*

He smiled at her, as if knowing her thoughts and promising that the strength would come.

"Then go, my love. My time here is done but you will give birth to my Kingdom."

"I will never go."

"And I will be with you always."

Now she wondered why he became smaller in her eyes, until she realized that she was walking away, backwards, unable to move her eyes from his face. When her body reached where it had been before it stopped, and there she stood, a lone sentinel in the wind.

How long she stood there she could not say. Others came, mocking him, insulting him; but to her they were just ghosts and shadows, and her only reality was the sight of Yeshua's face. He made no answer to his tormentors, but she knew the answer. It was in the sign above his head, and in his silence. His words came back to her: *My Kingdom is not of this world.* They did not understand, could not understand. But one day the whole world would know the meaning.

Then his body was wracked with spasms and blood flowed from his mouth. He lifted his eyes to heaven and cried, "My God! My God! Why have you forsaken me!?"

Then he looked at her, and she knew what he knew: he was not forsaken, would never be forsaken, as long as she lived.

And then he died.

It seemed to her that the world grew dark, and after that she could not say what she had done or where she had gone. In her mind she could only see him, and the last time she had looked in his eyes as he gazed upon the last thing he would see on Earth.

Chapter 22: Into the Earth

So on an afternoon before the Sabbath during one Passover, in the Prefecture of Pontius Pilate, under the reign of the Emperor Tiberius, the life and ministry of Yeshua of Nazareth ended.

A soldier confirmed his death and released his body for burial. In that last week it had been dangerous to support him when he was alive, but now that he was safely dead he could be as safely buried.

Yeshua had been a man for all people. If he extolled the virtues of the poor, he did not condemn the wealthy: unless they placed the gaining of wealth above virtue. If he promised Heaven to the powerless, he did not despise the powerful: unless they used their power for ill. He forgave sinners if they repented of their sins; he gave no quarter to hypocrites, who preached virtue but practiced vice. Even to the Romans he gave their due.

He had died friendless and alone, or so it had appeared. Now that it was too late for him but more safe for them, friends began to emerge from their lairs, blinking cautiously at the light. Some of these were rich men. Perhaps Yeshua would have spurned these men for being the hypocrites he despised. But then he must spurn all men, for who among them had stayed by his side at the end, even among the Twelve? In any case, the greater their wealth the greater their shame, for the same thoughts occurred to them.

His disciples had no land in Jerusalem. No doubt had they been pressed they would have rallied and found a place to lay their leader to his final rest. But they did not have to. Wealthy men came forward, and he was entombed in a new sepulcher in the slopes above the Valley of Hinnom. He was wrapped in a shroud infused with spices and oils and laid inside. Then a stone was rolled over the entrance to seal the tomb, to guard those outside from the stench of death and the body inside from the disgrace of attack by scavengers.

Word was sent to his disciples, so that they would know his fate and know where to pay whatever last respects they wished to give or monuments they wished to raise.

Then the sun went down and the Sabbath began, and finally the Lord rested from his labors.

CHAPTER 23: THE FLAMES OF GEHENNA

It was an hour past midnight when the two conspirators stole silently along the path toward the tomb. They did not speak, they kept to the shadows, and they walked as carefully as they could. It was unlikely anybody was among the tombs at this hour; unlikely anyone would suspect the sacrilege they were about to commit; but they had to be cautious. All hung on their deeds tonight.

They were fortunate. From the trees around they could see the moonlight shining on the clearing and the stone rolled across the tomb, and the area was empty of life. They looked at each other, and touched each other's hands. Their touch held a grief that would never die, and a resolve that would not be denied.

They moved quickly up to the stone, put their shoulders to it and heaved. It would not move. They found a large branch, placed it under the edge of the stone with a small stone under it, and pulled down on it with all their weight. Finally their groans were matched by a groaning from the stone, and with a loud grinding sound it rolled a few feet to the side, ending with a thump. They stood still for a moment, listening for sounds of alarm; but there was nothing but the sound of crickets and the lonely hoot of an owl. The black opening of the tomb beckoned.

They entered the tomb. The smell of spices was strong in the air; if the smell of decay had begun, they could not yet tell it. That was good; their task was hard enough without such finality. Working quickly, they lifted the body in its shroud and carried it out. Where it had lain they placed a fresh shroud, untouched by death.

They did not need to go far, but carrying a body was not easy. So they had brought an ass: the same ass that had carried Yeshua on his triumphant entry into Jerusalem, now carrying him unseen and unremarked except by the two walking silently beside it.

They had already prepared the site, nearby in Gehinnom down an overgrown trail. They had constructed a large nest of dry sticks and wood; they reverently placed the body on top of it and poured fragrant oil over the body and the wood. They had left hot embers here in a pot and now they added dry tinder and fanned them into flames. Then they lit the pyre, and watched as it burned.

He had already told her Yeshua's words on their last night together; words he had confirmed on the road to Calvary.

"It is not our way," Yeshua had said, "but our ways are not the only ways, and the Kingdom of God is for all men not just the Jews. Did not even some of our own kings meet their end in funeral fires? Shimon Kephas believes I am the Messiah, that I came to deliver Israel, and his faith will be sorely tested. He has ears, but has never heard. How many times have I said that the Kingdom of Heaven is not of this Earth? Only you, my friend, only you have understood; only you have the understanding and courage to carry out my will. When I die, my tomb must be empty. My body cannot be found. Only then will they believe the truth. Only then will they know what to do. So do this for me: you must rob my tomb, you must steal my body, you must consign it to fire. Then I will truly have escaped death, and ascended to my Father in Heaven."

And so they watched; and each cried their own tears for the man they had loved. As the fire grew its flickering flames reflected in their eyes, and the sparks and smoke rose into the sky. Yehuda whispered, "It is as he said. You remember, Miriam? This is where he said the damned would go. So now he burns in Gehinnom, descending into the depths of fiery Hell itself: but see! By descending into Hell, he also ascends into Heaven."

And as they watched, she reached out and took his hand. *And now the demons come for me again*, she thought. *Except they were not demons. I hated you, Yehuda, but I never stopped loving you.*

She remembered Yeshua's words, two nights ago that seemed a lifetime. *Miriam, love of my heart, my time is at an end. But yours is not. I know you love me. But you also love Yehuda. I see it in your eyes when you look at him; I see it in his, when he looks at you. For all that you have loved me, for all that you*

THE PASSION OF JUDAS

always will, you have never stopped loving him. I give him back to you, and you to him. One thing you must do for me. You will think it strange; you will not want to do it: yet you will want it more than you can know. On the night that I ascend to my Father in Heaven: on that night you must lay with Yehuda again. Do this, not despite me but in memory of me. To the others I give a sacrament of bread and wine; to the two of you I give one much greater. Swear that you will. Swear it on our love, all for all.

And so she had sworn.

Now as Yehuda looked at their clasped hands, then looked up to her face, with a sigh she reached for him and drew him to her; and they kissed, for the first time in years. Then the passion took them, and they lay together under the stars; and they made love as if it were their first time, in front of the flames that consumed the last mortal remains of Yeshua of Nazareth, that carried his sparks to the stars. And there was no guilt in it, for they did it in honor of themselves and of the man they had both loved.

And so they lay there, wrapped in each other, as the flames died down and the last sparks floated brief and lonely into the sky.

Then as the sky began to lighten, they arose, and scattered the ashes around and to the winds.

"Now go," he said to her. "You know what you must do. When your work is done, you know where you may find me. But if you never find me—know that I always loved you."

She glanced at him, startled first by his unexpected words then by the look of torture in his eyes. "But why…" she began, then stopped. She knew there would be no answer. *So many secrets, Yehuda. But soon I will know. I pray I can bear it, whatever it is that tortures you so.*

Yehuda had told her what Yeshua had asked of him, of the theft and burning: but she had to know that to do her part. Of the others' reasons for hanging him he would not speak, and she could not tell whether he wished to protect her, himself or the others. All he would say was, "You will know, Miriam. But not now. If you knew now you might not have the strength to do what must be done. Trust me, even if this is the last time."

Nor had she spoken with any of the others. Even as she watched her lord and love die on a cross among criminals, she had held herself apart, alone in her grief. The others had understood, or thought they did. But Yehuda had asked it of her and she had acquiesced; for though she yearned for the giving and receiving of comfort, she knew that there could be no comfort. Again she wondered what it was that he was so desperate for her not to know, but now was freeing her to learn.

Then he fled into the wilderness, and she made her way back to the empty tomb.

~~~

Miriam stood looking at the tomb as the sky lightened into dawn, the black opening of the cave staring back at her. *Here is your tomb, my love; but here you are no longer. You are no longer anywhere on Earth. Farewell, until we meet again in your Kingdom.*

She hurried off to where she knew Shimon Kephas would be; she found him there with Yaakov and Yohanan and called to them.

"Come! You must see!"

She gave them no opportunity to question her, just turned and hurried back the way she had come.

"Behold!"

The men looked at the open tomb. "What does this mean?"

"Look inside!"

They entered, then came out, faces ashen. "What does this mean? Tell us! Tell us all!"

Miriam had learnt the ways of Yeshua. She would tell the truth, in a way which would draw out a greater truth from the minds of the listeners. If it was not the literal truth, so be it.

"I came here at dawn and from afar there was a great flame rising to Heaven, and I was sorely afraid. Then when I came here I found the stone rolled away from the tomb. I found it empty. Except for his shroud, as empty as his tomb; as clean as if purified by the fiery hand of God."

"You saw no one?"

She hesitated. "There was one, but I know not what it means. You will not believe me. You will think me mad."

"Tell us!"

"There… there was a man. A young man. His eyes were like fire and his touch like flame. He told me that the man in the tomb was gone. That though he had died and descended into the fires of Hell, he has now arisen and ascended to be with his Father in Heaven."

The men looked at her, awestruck. On Shimon's face was something else as well; something like the look of deliverance. "Truly you are blessed among women, to be chosen to hear this! For surely the man you saw was an angel of the Lord!" he cried. "Come, we must tell the others!"

CHAPTER 24: THE ROAD

Two men walked along a dusty road leading west from Jerusalem. The sun was hot and the slight breeze did little to remove its heat, but they did not notice. They were intently discussing the events of the morning, in tones alternating between skepticism and excitement. Then they heard the scuff of sandals behind them and turned to look.

There was a stranger following them, dark eyes watching them out of a face otherwise largely covered. They had not heard him come and did not know where he had come from. They did not know him, but neither could shake the feeling that there was something familiar about him. They had the same feeling when he spoke, though his voice was one they had not heard before: it was hoarse and whispery, as though its bearer was ancient of days, even though they could tell he was only around their own age; perhaps like them he had merely seen more than most men had or wanted to.

"What is this you speak of, strangers?" the man had asked.

"You come from Jerusalem, and you do not know? We speak of the death of Yeshua, the great Prophet from Nazareth."

"Forgive me, but I heard you speaking of life not death."

The two looked at each nervously. Whether they were nervous of a spy or merely of being thought mad, perhaps they were not sure themselves. But they remembered the events of which they spoke, and their courage rose to what such events demanded.

"You speak truly, stranger. We have heard an amazing thing! Though he died, and was buried, the woman who went to his tomb this morning discovered it empty! And an Angel of the Lord appeared to her there, saying he had risen, and been taken up to his Father in Heaven!"

"Then you are fools."

"Why do you say that?" one replied angrily. "It is as we say!"

"I have no doubt of it. You are fools not for believing it, but for not believing it."

"What do you mean?"

"Did not this Yeshua tell you himself that he would die and rise to Heaven? That he came to bring his Father's Kingdom, but that Kingdom was not of this Earth? Where then should he go, when his Kingdom came?"

They looked at him, open mouthed.

"If you did not understand him, do you not understand the Scriptures? Attend me well, men."

Then he explained to them the hints, clues and prophecies in the Scriptures, which foretold the coming of a man who would be Messiah yet not King: a man who would die then rise again to be seated, not among the kings of Earth but at the right hand of their Heavenly Father Himself. A King who came, not to rule men but to save them.

By the time he had finished they had reached their destination, the village of Emmaus.

"Who are you, stranger?" one of them asked.

"It does not matter who I am. All that matters is who Yeshua is. So think carefully on my words, for now I must leave you. I have my own destination to reach."

"Oh, no, stranger! It is late! Stay with us tonight instead."

"Very well."

When they went into the place they were staying the stranger said, "In return for your hospitality I will prepare the meal. Go, rest from your travels, which have been hard; come down when you will."

And so, weary from their travels and the events of the past days, they did. But when they came down, they saw bread and wine set for them on the table; the bread broken as Yeshua had in their last supper together, the wine poured likewise. As if one who had been present had done it. But the stranger had vanished.

They looked at each other, amazed.

And came to their own conclusions.

CHAPTER 25: THE ROCK

Yehuda sat on a rock, casting small stones into the wilderness like so many times before. Only now he was truly alone; now his life was riven by loss and grief.

He had done his last task for Yeshua on the day they had sent him to his Father. He had watched, knowing some opportunity would be had, and then when two of the disciples had left Jerusalem he had taken it. He had disguised himself again and gone to join them. Since that day he had waited in his lonely wilderness redoubt.

Nobody bothered him. If any travelers saw him, all they saw was another mystic or ascetic serving his time in the wilderness. Approaching one of those was an invitation to a harangue or begging, so any who diverged from their path were more likely to veer away than closer. If anyone did approach seeking wisdom he would soon disabuse them of the notion he had any. None did.

As he had done so many times in the hours and days before, he found himself looking at the landscape and assessing its potential for deposits of fine clays or colored minerals. He was not seriously thinking about these things. His last few years had been like riding a powerful stallion, then suddenly he had been thrown from it. He could lie in the dust and die, or rebuild himself piece by piece. So he found himself retreating into the protective shell of his former life; not as serious steps but more like the start of a promise. *I will find a town, find a wife to bear my children, and be as any other man. One day I may look back on these days with wonder for what we did. One day, when my heart is healed. If it ever is.*

As he had thought every day before in the past week, he decided that tomorrow he would leave for that new life. Miriam had not returned; he knew she would never return. At least she had not led the others to him. *What is this loyalty she shows me, again and again, in the face of my betrayals? But I cannot trust her forever. I cannot wait forever for one who will never come. So I will go. Tomorrow.*

He watched one of the rare groups of travellers crossing his domain, just normal people going in the same direction and keeping together for company and protection. Out of automatic caution he drew his *sicara* and placed it within easy reach behind the rock he sat on. But while they were close enough to see they were far enough that they would not bother him, with nothing but a few incurious glances cast his way to show they were even aware of his existence. But then one of them stopped to let the others pass before turning aside to move toward him.

It was a young woman, and though his heart seemed to stop in his throat he watched her approach with an air of no more than idle interest. He would have run to her, but there was something strange about her. Though she could see his eyes upon her she showed no eagerness; she walked slowly, as if reluctant to join him. Yet she came straight toward him, as if no other destination mattered to her.

Finally she came to a stop just in front of him, searching his face with her eyes.

"Miriam."

But she did not return his welcome. Instead she looked at him as if not knowing what it was she saw. Or as one would look at a snake.

"Is it true?" she asked in a voice of desperation and grief. "Why, Yehuda? Why?"

"If you believe it, why did you come?" he asked harshly, now refusing to meet her gaze.

She drew her knife from under her tunic and replied in a voice so low it was almost a growl, "So that if it is true, I may kill you myself."

He showed her his own weapon so she could see its deadly form, holding it straight out toward her heart. "You come to me, a woman, alone in this wilderness, bringing nothing but accusations and a blade? Do you wish to die too?"

"Would you slay me, Yehuda?" she asked softly. "Would you slay me too?"

She moved slowly toward him until the point of his blade dug into the flesh over her heart. "Then slay me," she said in a whisper both hoarse and trembling, her eyes searching his for something she knew would not be found.

He saw contempt and fear warring in her eyes; and a third emotion, one that seemed unable to accept that those could exist between the two of them, and not caring to remain in a world where they were possible.

His own eyes flashed and he leapt to his feet, drawing his sword back then plunging its point into the ground at his feet. "I would die first!" he cried.

Then he sat again, and looked up at her.

"No, Miriam. It is not true."

"But they confronted you! They found the silver! Why, Yehuda, why, why, why?"

"It was not I."

"Why should I believe you?! If you betrayed him, no lie would be beyond you!"

"I swear it. I swear it by…" *By what, Yehuda? Your honor? Your love? What can you swear by, that could ever be enough?* "I swear by Yahweh Himself, by Lord God Almighty, God of Israel, Father of Yeshua; I swear by all I have ever loved; I swear by my own life."

She stared at him, startled. If he would dare name their God, swear by that terrible name: he was either more damned than she could have imagined, or innocent. She searched his face, seeking the shifting eyes of a liar or a coward. But all she could see was a desperate sincerity, shocking in its naked appeal.

"But… they found your blood money on you! If not you, then who?"

For long seconds he did not speak. Then he asked quietly, "Who found the silver?"

"You know Kephas found it in your belongings."

His eyes bored into hers, daring her to see what he had seen. When he saw her eyes begin to darken in shock, he answered their unspoken horror.

"Yes. Kephas."

It was if the name had dropped into a deep well between them, never finding its bottom. For more seconds than they could remember neither of them spoke, until finally Miriam shook herself as if from a dream.

"It is impossible! Kephas is the last man on Earth who would betray Yeshua!"

"So you would think. So we would all think."

"Why do you accuse him?! If you have the proof—why did you not denounce him?"

Yehuda sighed. "I think I knew at the time, but I could not believe it either. But I have been thinking about it and the pattern is clear. I had never seen that silver before: yet Kephas found it in my bag. Only he did not find it: he had it with him. And before that, just after I kissed Yeshua in the Garden and those men appeared, I saw Kephas pointing at us with a look of horror. I thought he was pointing at the strangers and the horror was of them. I was wrong. He was pointing at Yeshua, so there would be no mistake, and the horror was at his own act."

"But it makes no sense! Why?"

"Because he believed too much and too deeply. He could not understand why Yeshua would not declare his Kingdom. He believed that if only he were delivered into the hands of his enemies, he must finally declare himself the Messiah; for he was the Messiah, and if he were threatened the very angels of Heaven must come to his aid.

"That is why it nearly destroyed him. Yeshua would not fight. No angels came to his aid. Yeshua was destroyed. And Shimon is the one who caused it. Did you see his eyes that night? How he bore it, I can never know."

"But why accuse you? Why murder you?"

"Again: did you see his eyes? No man could long bear what he bore. He could not believe what he had done; could not afford to believe he had done it. He had tried to force the birth of the Kingdom of Heaven: instead he had killed the man he loved the most. It could not have been him: it had to be someone else. It might as well be me: on one hand the outsider from Kerioth he had never liked, on the other hand his rival, the man Yeshua had known as a boy."

"That does not justify what he did!"

"It was his madness that did it. The betrayer could not have been him: so it must have been me. But even in the depths of his madness, some glimmer of Shimon remained. He tied the noose loosely. I would have died, but he gave me time. It was enough."

"But he still did it! Why do you hide here in the wilderness? Why do you not denounce him and clear yourself?"

"Tell me, Miriam: how goes Shimon now? How are the others?"

"He is... changed. He has leapt upon Yeshua's vision of a Kingdom of the Spirit like a man possessed, like one who sees a mighty lion and does not run but seizes it by the mane to ride it. He inspires the others. They would have followed Yeshua into Hell itself. Now they follow Kephas into the Kingdom of Heaven."

She paused, looking at Yehuda with wide eyes.

"It has begun."

He nodded.

"Then you know why. Yeshua told me the Rock had to break. That when he broke, if a way out were opened to him he would take it and be refined into a mighty force. Shifting his blame to me was his own solution to reducing the forces crushing him. But in the end it made the pressure worse: two betrayals in place of one."

"Do you think Yeshua knew? That Shimon would betray him?"

Yehuda picked up his *sicara* and ran its point in patterns through the soil at his feet. Then he said quietly, "I think it was his idea."

He looked up at her shocked face.

"You know how he was. You recall his cryptic remarks. What he told Shimon in private we cannot know, but I think he wove the tapestry together in a way that planted the idea in Shimon's head. Yeshua had to make sure. The shock of his arrest and death might have been enough; but perhaps not. Add to that Kephas himself being the cause: well, you have seen it. But it had to be his own idea so he would feel the full force of his own guilt."

"However, one thing Yeshua did not foresee," he added with a mirthless smile. "He did not imagine Kephas would try to kill me. It was fortunate you were there. Or perhaps that also was part of his plan. So that someone would be there if the unexpected happened."

"But now the man who betrayed Yeshua leads his people!"

"He is the only one who can do it. The others are all good men. But they are not Kephas. Without him, it would go on, fading day by day until the day it dissolves in some trackless wilderness and Yeshua and his words are finally forgotten."

"But Yehuda! His name will be blessed for all generations! While yours will be mud! You will be accursed by all men, to the end of time!"

Then she stopped, a look of shock on her face, and she cried, "And what about me!? You never told me! You let me go there, knowing what they would say! Knowing I must believe them! Knowing I might never come back! I would have... I would have never seen you again!

I would have spent the rest of my life hating you! Every memory of you... everything we ever shared... poisoned by betrayal! Yehuda! Why? How?"

"You had to go back, knowing nothing. I knew you would not betray our secret, but how could you bear another? Could you have been with them, sharing their meals, watching what Kephas was becoming, watching the others turning to him in their hour of need—knowing what he had done? What would happen if they knew too?"

"It would tear them apart. It would be over. They would never recover."

"And so they must think it was me."

"But now you are damned in their eyes for all time! And the more Kephas succeeds the more damned you will be!"

"Miriam, Yeshua talked to me once of price. That everything has a price, one we must choose to pay or not. What is the price of my good name compared to the price Yeshua was willing to pay? If my name is to be damned to the end of time for his Kingdom to be born, then for him I will pay it. Miriam, you cannot know how desperately I hoped I would not lose you. But if I am to lose the one woman I love for that Kingdom to be born, then so be it. I would have died for him! I would die for you even if you were to damn me with your own lips to all eternity!"

"Miriam," he added more softly, "I sent you to them, knowing you would probably not come back, knowing you might betray me to the others. Knowing you might never know the truth, that I might never see you again, that you would hate and despise me to the end of your days. That the lie you believed true would hurt you too, too deeply for forgiveness: and I couldn't stand it. But for Yeshua, I would have done even that."

"You loved him that much?" she whispered.

"I loved him that much."

And then she sat beside him on his rock, and held his hand between hers, and wept.

Epilogue

Three Months Later

Yehuda stood on a hill overlooking the port city of Caesarea. Somewhere down there was Pontius Pilate, the man who had condemned Yeshua to die; but Yehuda knew he was not truly to blame. Perhaps he could have saved Yeshua, but why would he? He meant no more to Pilate than Pilate meant to Yehuda.

Miriam stood beside him on the hill looking down on the city and at the sparkling, restless sea beyond. "So this is Kesariya. Soon we leave."

"Yes."

"Have you thought where we shall go?"

"Far towards the setting sun. I think Greece for now. They are a civilized people with a gentle climate. There we will be safe. After that, who knows? I am thinking further west, perhaps Hispania or Gaul. I wonder how long it will be before someone brings us the Good News of Yeshua? I wonder what we should say to them, if they do."

Miriam was silent for a minute, lost in her own contemplation.

They had travelled for weeks now. They were neither hiding nor fleeing, but steadily making their way to their destination. They needed to worry only about that destination.

On the day after she returned to him and learned the truth, Miriam had told him what else the others were saying about him.

"They seem to think your betrayal wasn't enough to damn you. Now practically everything you said or did gains a dark motive. And you are now a thief too. When they came back and found the money entrusted to you, they said a lot was missing. Not all, but about a third of what they had thought should be there. They conclude you have been stealing from us for a long time, though I'm not sure what they think it is you were spending it on. So what is the truth, Yehuda? Where did it go?"

"That money was Yeshua's to dispose of. He told me to take it, that we would need it on our journey. So I hid it, and now I have it. I feared I would spend it alone. I am glad I will be spending it with you. But it is not for wealth. We need to travel a long distance, and cannot be left destitute needing to work every step of the way. So it is enough: for food, for lodging, for transport, until we can settle and start a new life."

Settle and start a new life, she thought. *It sounds so simple. It is so simple. Yet it is something I never thought I would hear.* Then she had cried tears that were the summation of all the years of past and future, and he had held her close for a long time.

And here they were, she thought as they stood together on a hill, about to start the longest but not the greatest journey of her life.

~~~

"Do you think he can do it?" she asked at last. "Kephas? Do you really think he can fulfill Yeshua's dream?"

Yehuda smiled. "I think so. He's the only one who's a big enough bastard to do it!"

"And if he does? What will happen?"

"Even Yeshua could not see that. You know his words had power. You know his message was of peace and the love of man for man. But you have also seen the dark side. You know what men can do, to words and each other. I pray for Yeshua's sake that his vision is preserved. If not—perhaps some of it will be preserved. And perhaps that will be enough."

She smiled, and gently patted the small bump on her belly. He smiled too, and placed his hand over hers.

"And this child growing inside me," she said softly. "I wonder if it is Yeshua's: or yours? I wonder if he somehow knew; if that was one of his reasons for asking me to do what we did that night. So that no one could ever know?"

"It does not matter. It is his, and it is mine, and it is ours. That is all that matters to me in the world."

HISTORICAL NOTES

L ittle is known about the real life of Jesus and his disciples, or even if they lived at all, as hard evidence is lacking. The only sources are the Gospels of the New Testament themselves, but even the earliest fragments we have were written decades after the events. While there are numerous other Gospels (the apocryphal or non-canonical Gospels), even the Church did not accept them as genuine, and the stories in them tend to be wilder and less plausible.

While there are mentions by independent historians such as Josephus, their sources were most likely the Christians themselves so they cannot truly be regarded as independent sources.

To add to the confusion all of the authors, whether Gospel writers or historians, had their own agendas to advance: none can be considered disinterested observers. Rather they are players in their own dramas.

However none of that proves the story is a myth: even Pontius Pilate, who as Roman Prefect could be expected to have more records during his lifetime than Jesus and his followers, has little evidence to his name. But such evidence as we do have, notably a stone inscription bearing his name, proves he did exist and had the role of Prefect as described in the Gospels.

That said, the Gospels read like any non-believing reader would expect: collections of anecdotes, not necessarily consistent, not necessarily accurate and likely to be exaggerated: as is the nature of tales about exciting events. If I thought the Gospels were the literal Word of God, this novel would not exist: the Bible would do. But this novel starts from the premise that the Gospels were the work of men: and that Jesus himself was a man, albeit an extraordinary one.

The historian's pain is the novelist's gain: varying versions of events give latitude in what story we tell, while complete holes allow our imagination to drive through the gaps. So what is history, what is interpretation, and what is imagination?

This novel largely ignores the apocryphal Gospels (of which there are a surprising number, including ones attributed to Mary Magdalene and Judas themselves). That is simply because they tend to be even more fanciful and clearly written to advance a particular agenda than the canonical ones. However they are not entirely ignored, merely taken with a much larger grain of salt. For perhaps they too record some truth.

The story of Mary Magdalene (Miriam of Magdala) is key to this novel, and her life has been the subject of contradictory speculations or dogma for centuries. In the Bible she is variously described as one of the women who supported Jesus with her wealth, a woman from whom Jesus had cast out seven demons, one of the witnesses to the crucifixion, and the first person to witness the resurrection of Jesus. The apocryphal Gospels describe her as even closer, with the Gospel of Philip calling her Jesus' "companion" and other Gospels stressing her importance as a disciple or even "apostle to the apostles".

Yet Mary Magdalene is not mentioned in the Bible by name outside of the Gospels or even after the resurrection. She is not mentioned by Paul or in any other of the Epistles that make up the New Testament. But she clearly paid an important role, given how often she is mentioned in the Gospels and that in the Gospel of John she is named as the only witness to the resurrection. Then after that critical event she vanishes entirely from the record.

There is no evidence that Mary was the prostitute Jesus forgave nor the woman caught in adultery whom Jesus saved from stoning. However both those stories have powerful messages; both could have been told as stories in their own right. Thus in this story Mary is not a prostitute, but she is the adulteress saved from stoning. The story of the demons and the story of the adultery are the same story, filtered through different mouths, recombined as separate fragments in the Gospels.

Other than the towns they came from, no real back story is given in the Bible for either Mary Magdalene or Judas Iscariot, other than the unexplained facts that Mary was a woman of means and Judas was chosen to handle the money. How, when or where they came to join Jesus' band is not revealed. Their histories as told here are entirely my invention.

While to avoid confusion most place names mentioned in this novel retain the forms familiar to modern readers, to add historical flavor most personal names are rendered more closely to their original forms as spoken at the time. The chief changes are that in Greek and Latin there was no "J", only "I" serving as both the vowel and the consonant (as a consonant it was pronounced like "Y"—so it was much like "Y" itself in English)—and the letter "s" was usually added to the end of male names. Furthermore, in the Old Testament the names are closer to the original while in the New Testament they are more like their Greek or Latin forms. Thus "Yeshua" is written "Joshua" in the Old Testament and becomes "Jesus" in the New, while "Yehuda" evolves to "Judah" and then to our "Judas".

Following is a glossary of important names, terms and places. Where appropriate this lists the names in the form used in this novel along with their form as they appear in the Bible, along with any historical and other explanatory notes.

GLOSSARY OF NAMES

Abba: Father, often in a familiar sense analogous to "dad" or "daddy".

Akhilleus: Achilles, a mighty hero of ancient Greek legend who fought in the Trojan War. In *The Iliad* it is said he faced two choices: to be a hero who dies young, never to return home; or to go home, live long, and be forgotten. He chose glory and we still remember his name.

Andreas: Andrew, the apostle Peter's older brother. Andreas is a Greek name with no Hebrew precursor (Greek culture had a large influence in Galilee by the time of Jesus and purely Greek names were not uncommon).

Barabbas: A contraction of Bar Abbas, "Son of Abbas". A notorious robber, condemned to die, but according to the New Testament pardoned by demand of the crowd in place of Jesus. The robber Abbas, hinted to be his father by both name and occupation, is an invention of this novel.

Binyamin: Benjamin. A common Jewish name and one of the original tribes of Israel.

El Shaddai: One of the early Hebrew names for God, literally "God Almighty".

Eliyahu: Elijah, a famous prophet in the era of the Kings of Israel. According to the Bible he did not die but was taken up to heaven in a fiery chariot by a whirlwind, and his return was prophesied by the later prophet Malachi.

Gehinnom (Greek: Gehenna): the Valley of Hinnom, southwest of ancient Jerusalem. Notorious in the Old Testament as the place where children were burned in sacrifice to Moloch and used by Jesus as a metaphor for Hell and its eternal fires (the word translated to "Hell" in the Gospels is usually Gehenna). The slopes of the Hinnom Valley were used for tombs by the wealthiest Jewish families in the first century. The actual location of the tomb of Jesus (and even where he was crucified) are debated, but as the Gospels say Jesus was buried by wealthy men, Gehinnom is a plausible location, and the symbolism of his burial there made it an obvious one for this novel.

Gentiles: non-Jews. In Judaism the Jews are God's chosen people and other peoples are gentiles (Hebrew goyim). Christianity was non-exclusive (though this was not without debate at the time) and preached to Jew and Gentile alike.

Gospels: literally, "Good News", namely the Good News about Jesus Christ. The four "canonical Gospels"—Matthew, Mark, Luke and John—are so called because they were named by the early Church as the ones that spoke the truth. But there are many apocryphal Gospels as well, also attributed to eyewitnesses at the time (including Mary Magdalene and Judas) though written decades after the events.

Hasmodean: a dynasty of Jewish kings founded after the successful rebellion of the Maccabees against the Seleucid Empire (see Yehuda HaMakabi).

Herod the Great (Herod I). A Roman client king of Judea, who defeated the last of the Hasmonean kings and set up his own dynasty. On his death in 4 BCE the kingdom was divided among his sons including Herod Antipas.

Herod Antipas: Tetrarch of Galilee (tetrarch means quarter-king, so called because it was rule over only one part of the whole province) in the time of Jesus. According to the Gospels he imprisoned John the Baptist when John criticized his marriage, and later was maneuvered into beheading him by his wife: who took advantage of his promise to her daughter, generally identified as Salome, after he offered her a reward for her dancing.

Hinnom, Valley of: See Gehinnom.

Kanai: Zealot. A member of the Zealots, a Jewish political movement seeking to expel Rome from Israel by force of arms. Also see Shimon Kanai.

Kesariya: Caesarea Maritima, a Roman port city on the upper western coast of Israel. It was the seat of the Roman Prefect and a major Mediterranean port.

Ketubbah: a Jewish marriage contract, especially the settlement the wife is to receive upon divorce or her husband's death.

Kyrene: Cyrene, an ancient Greek and Roman city in Libya, home to a significant Jewish minority. According to the Gospels, Simon of Cyrene was compelled to carry Jesus' cross.

Mattithyahu: Matthew. Formerly a tax collector, one of the 12 Disciples and reputedly the author of the Gospel of Matthew.

Messiah: Christ. Literally "Anointed One", after the practice of declaring someone King by anointing his head with oil. When under the rule of foreign nations, the Jews would hope for such a one to come: their true king who would liberate them from their oppressors and restore the Jewish Kingdom.

Miriam: Mary. Miriam was the most common name of Jewish women in the first century AD. There are a number of women named Mary in the Gospels including Jesus' own mother and Mary Magdalene.

Miriam the Hasmodean (also: Mariamne I): A Hasmonean princess and the second wife of Herod the Great.

Pharisees: one of the important Jewish political and religious factions in the time of Jesus. Often wealthy businessmen, they were more in touch with and enjoyed greater support from the common people than their rivals, the Sadducees. They shared many of Jesus' beliefs such as the authority of the Old Testament including the prophets, and the resurrection of the dead. However Jesus was opposed to their adherence to oral tradition and ritualistic exactitude, and they were united with the Sadducees in their opposition to him. After the destruction of the Temple in 70 AD, their beliefs became the basis of rabbinic Judaism as it is still mostly practiced today.

Robber: As opposed to thieves, who stole by stealth, robbers stole openly by armed force. The authorities would call someone a robber whether he preyed on everyone or only on the Romans. So a robber to the authorities may well have been a hero to the local people; thus being analogous to Robin Hood, Resistance fighters or guerillas. This explains why the Jews would have asked for the release of Barabbas.

Sadducees: the second important Jewish political and religious faction in the time of Jesus. Unlike the Pharisees they were aristocratic and favored many Greek ideas, and they also denied the authority of the prophets, an afterlife and the existence of angels and demons. They were more concerned with politics than religion and sought accommodation with the Romans. They united with the Pharisees against Jesus when they began to fear he would attract the attention and ire of Rome. Unlike the Pharisees, the Sadducees ceased to exist after the destruction of the Temple in 70 AD.

Samaritans: the descendants of Israelites who remained in northern Israel during the Babylonian exile. Tensions between them and the returned exiles survive even to this day, with both groups claiming to hold the genuine faith of their ancestors.

Sanhedrin: The Jewish ruling council, comprised mainly of Pharisees and Sadducees. Each city had a lesser Sanhedrin of 23 men, with the Great Sanhedrin of 71 men in Jerusalem acting something like our national government and supreme court, though in Jesus' time subject to Rome.

Sea of Galilee: also known as the Lake of Gennesaret or Lake Tiberius. The largest freshwater lake in Israel, about 13 miles long and 8 miles wide with a maximum depth of about 140 feet. It is in northeast Israel and fed mainly by the Jordan River, flowing through it from north to south. It was home to an extensive fishing industry.

Shelomit: Salome. The second most common female name in first century Judea after Miriam. Salome the disciple of Jesus is mentioned only briefly in the gospels as one of the witnesses to the crucifixion and resurrection. That Salome is unrelated to the daughter of Herodias, traditionally identified as Salome, whose dancing before Herod Antipas led to the death of John the Baptist. Her back story in this novel as a reformed prostitute is my invention.

Sheol: the Jewish underworld, comparable to Hades in Greek mythology, where the dead resided.

Shimon: Simon. A common name among men in Roman Judea, and several characters in the Gospels share this name and are distinguished by surnames or nicknames (e.g. Kephas) or alternate spelling (e.g. Simeon).

Shimon Kanai: Simon Zealotes, or Simon the Zealot, one of the Twelve Disciples. See Kanai.

Shimon Kephas: Simon Peter. Kephas (Aramaic) and Peter (Greek) mean "Rock". Foremost of the Twelve Disciples and important founder of the Christian Church.

Sicara: a dagger with a curved blade. The Sicarii were assassins named after the blade. Contrary to some theories the name Judas Iscariot does not refer to the Sicarii, and Yehuda's use of a sicara in this story is purely coincidental.

Teoma (meaning "twin"): Thomas, one of the apostles. Known as "Doubting Thomas" for the story in John's gospel where he refused to believe in Jesus' resurrection until he could see and feel it for himself.

Yaakov: Jacob: James. The Yaakov in this story is the son of Zebedee, brother of Yohanan (John), also known as James the Greater. He is distinct from two other disciples named James: James the son of Alphaeus, also called James the Lesser (the Greater and Lesser probably refer to physical stature) and James the Just, brother of Jesus. The last was not among the original disciples but came to prominence after Jesus' death (though the Roman Catholic Church regards him and the Lesser James as the same man). The brothers James and John were given the Hebrew nickname Bene Reghesh, "Sons of Rage", paraphrased into the Greek Boanerges, "Sons of Thunder": from which we can estimate their personalities.

Yahweh: the Hebrew personal name for God. Taking that name in vain (swearing by it falsely) was a capital offence, and it was so holy that even mentioning it outside a formal oath was to be avoided.

Yehuda: Judas. In the Old Testament it is written as Judah and is the name of one of the Twelve Tribes of Israel, and thence became the name of the part of Israel they controlled. The Roman name for the province, Judea or Judaea, is a Latin transliteration of Judah.

Yehuda HaMakabi: Judas Maccabeus. He led the Maccabean Revolt against the Seleucid Empire (167–160 BCE). See Hasmodean.

Yehuda of Kerioth: Judas Iscariot. The surname is from the Hebrew "Ish Kerioth" meaning Man of Kerioth, a town in southern Judea. The name is unrelated to the Sicarii, assassins whose weapon was traditionally the sicara.

Yeshua: Jesus. In the Old Testament it is written as Joshua and was the name of the leader who brought the Israelites into Canaan after Moses' death. A very common name among first century Jews and of course made famous by Jesus of Nazareth.

Yirmeyahu: Jeremiah, a major prophet of the Old Testament, famous for castigating the Jews for turning away from their true God and explaining their impending destruction and captivity by the Babylonians. He suffered much for his unpopular prophecies.

Yohanan: John. A common name in first century Judea and the name of John the Baptist and John the disciple of Jesus.

About the Author

Dr Robin Craig has a PhD in molecular biology and a keen interest in science and philosophy. He believes that novels, like all art, should be one in thought, theme and style: to nourish the mind as much as the soul. His books specialize in blending fact and speculation in dramatic and engaging stories, driven by strong characters and intriguing, topical philosophical themes.

In addition to near future science fiction exploring contemporary issues such as artificial intelligence (*Frankensteel*), genetic engineering (*The Geneh War*) and cyborg technology (*Time Enough for Killing*), his books include time travel (*The Time Surgeons*), alternative history (*The Passion of Judas*) and a collection of short stories (*Past, Present, Future*).

He also writes non-fiction. In addition to 14 scientific papers and a long-running philosophical series in *TableAus* (the journal of Australian Mensa), he has published numerous philosophical essays on Amazon.com and was a contributor to *The Australian Book of Atheism* with his chapter *Good Without God*, an essay on the importance and validity of secular ethics.

Dr Craig is an independent author. If you like this book please spread the word with reviews and recommendations to your friends or library... and enjoy more of his books!

To keep up to date on new and upcoming works and events, follow his Facebook page at fb.me/authorcraig.

www.ingramcontent.com/pod-product-compliance
Lightning Source LLC
Chambersburg PA
CBHW031949130726
47904CB00012B/955